TALES FROM GRANDAD

TIME TRAVEL

DON KEIRLE

authorHOUSE®

AuthorHouse™ UK
1663 Liberty Drive
Bloomington, IN 47403 USA
www.authorhouse.co.uk
Phone: 0800.197.4150

Published by AuthorHouse 03/29/2016

ISBN: 978-1-5246-3076-8 (sc)
ISBN: 978-1-5246-3077-5 (hc)
ISBN: 978-1-5246-3078-2 (e)

Print information available on the last page.

Any people depicted in stock imagery provided by Thinkstock are models,
and such images are being used for illustrative purposes only.
Certain stock imagery © Thinkstock.

This book is printed on acid-free paper.

CHAPTER 1

THINKING BEGINS.

Helen Svensson had successfully deviated from thinking about time travel whilst in the earlier times of her theories about the rethe. At the time, she had needed such a sharp focus on the perceived problems of that era that she had refused to let the seed that was in her mind, grow at all.

This same seed was in the Whistler's mind too. He too had been preoccupied with the problems in hand, and had simply archived the notion away. Its embryo surfaced now and then, but he had been able to quell it easily.

The world was now in another phase of its development generally referred to as 'the reformation'. The major victory after the recent upheavals was to graft decent ideas into the minds of the political animals. These animals would never be able to keep to the straight and narrow as none of them had and would always lack what folk called 'common sense'. However for the moment the world was wobbling its unsteady way generally in the right direction.

The economic climate was slowly turning upwards and optimism was rising. The Space administration still had plenty of funding. After Helen had finally sorted through all of the claims of Space centre employees back pay, the whole organisation was beginning to function in a fashion that the Whistler thought of as 'normal'.

As the director for Space research, James Whistler needed a big project to occupy the minds and time of his people. Robot development was coming along nicely and a number of his top men were busily engaged in the design of them. The long term aim was to be able to leave a team of robots functioning on planets and or moons, where no man could survive, and generally to advance the frontiers of knowledge into the bargain. Though these projects were massive enough, they did not occupy the spaceman branch of his enterprises. The spaceman branch's activities brought in rewards, whereas the robot arm of his enterprise had sights set far into the future and were not part of a general commercial function.

This was a sunny morning in June, James Whistler hummed as he walked from the carpark into his laboratory. He greeted Helen Svensson as she walked across the carpark from its opposite end. "Morning Helen, have you got an itch that needs scratching?"

"Morning James, sure have. Probably the same one that you have, if you've got the time?!" she quipped, as they hurried along.

Up in Helen's office, the lap tops were swiftly opened and Helen admitted whilst revisiting her work files on the rethe, "I knew I wouldn't be able to leave time travel alone for much longer. The idea is lurking away in the back of my mind, and I almost mentioned it yesterday."

"Same for me. We need a major project to occupy the Space service but, we mustn't let the idea of it get out to the public otherwise we will find ourselves losing out to the reckless characters again. What can we call it?"

Helen then smiled and said "I have pondered that myself, and my first though was to call it the 'emit' project. But that was a bit too easy for the speculators to decode so I thought about the 'reconciliation time' project."

James Whistler pursed his lips and then added "we do have a problem reconciling the journey times of some of our later flights that is true. We did in essence go boldly forth, but we lost control over exactly what we were doing, and as a result of that we have results to worry about when we have no idea what forces were involved in the creation of the time anomalies. This is the fault of no-one. I really don't think our knowledge is advanced enough for us to have proceeded other than the way we actually did at the time.

What I propose is that both of us handle the projects and issues that come our way, but we must adjust our calendars to set aside perhaps a quarter of our time to considering time travel. This will of course involve a root and branch re-examination of all of the data at our disposal!"

"Coffee?" she enquired and he nodded in the affirmative.

"Reconciliation Anomalies. The R.A. project!" he beamed. "That is true in so far as it is the time anomalies that we are trying to account for, but we can talk openly with a title like that, and it would be easy to effect another explanation if any curious news hounds appear on the scene!" he sipped his coffee.

Helen smiled and said "Consider this then. It is known that we have successfully alloyed lead and aluminium in Space, something that can only be done under zero gravity conditions due to the disparity in the densities of the constituent parts. Fortunately, that particular alloy has no known exceptional properties, and it attracts no real interest, so if we go along that line, once again we will attract no interest. The idea could be considered worth pursuing. The long diamond shards are still a playing a large and useful part in any industry that manufacture parts requiring physical strength. So we could ostensibly be conducting research into useful materials like those I just mentioned, and even produce something to show for it whilst the real motive for our work is well disguised!"

"What a clever wench you are! The time modulated alloy project" he grinned happily, and then glanced at his watch, leaped from his chair and said "Ok, shuffle your calendar around and I will talk to you as soon as I get the chance. I'm already late for the latest board meeting. See you later!"

The big brains of the Space Administration were not, however, the only ones who were intrigued by certain possibilities.

CHAPTER 2

HELEN'S OTHER HALF PONDERS

Henrik Svensson knew he didn't have the shear intuitive deductive powers of his wife, but he was no fool. She sometimes mumbled in her sleep, and he realised from this that something was afoot, and it started him thinking of something that had lain dormant at the back of his mind for some while now.

He cast his mind back to the speck of dirt incident where a speck on his computor screen had been interpreted as a decimal point. He remembered how they had had to wait out in Space for what seemed an interminable time for the auto programmed ship to exit the rethe. He now further wondered what would happen if the rocket motors were kept at full thrust as the jump was made. If Helens inverse time theory was true this would mean a zero time element into her equations which should then be expressed as spending an infinite amount of ether time before reappearance was made. In other words, lost for ever.

The Space missions subsequently undertaken had all used an ether time element suited to an arbitrary decision by Captain Johnson. This decision was based purely on time required aboard the spaceships to carry out the necessary safety checks with five minutes added just for good measure.

He wondered what would happen if say two ships went on a mission and jumped into the rethe and one spent say five minutes in there whilst the other spent ten minutes there.

They should exit the rethe on the same heading but at different times, so would they be able to communicate or would they even be able to detect each other? If they headed for the precise same spot, would one ship suddenly exit the rethe and find itself inextricably intertwined with the other or what? He decided he would talk to Helen the following morning at breakfast, and fell into a troubled sleep.

The following morning Henrik decided to have a good old English fry up.

He had the bacon grilling and the eggs in the pan when Helen stumbled blearily down stairs. Henrik took one look at her and began to titter. He put his pan onto the stove and turned the gas down, and then burst into uncontrolled mirth.

She had a half smile on her face but was mystified as to what had set him off. Until she saw herself, in the mirror. Her hair raven black, usually an elegantly styled example of how hair should look, had the look of a trampled beehive.

"It isn't that funny!" she grumbled, "and it's better than your straggly blond mess!"

"Quite true" he said grinning widely "fried bread?"

"I suppose it doesn't hurt once in a while, but go easy on the black pudding!" she shot off to fix her hair. She really was lucky. Her hair had always been lustrous and glossy and took only seconds to straighten out. She dropped onto her stool in the kitchen and began to wolf down her breakfast. "You aren't preggers again are you?" asked Henrik.

She shook her head in the negative saying "no but I've got a raging appetite, you know!"

"Ah, it must be work then!" he shot a glance at her, and knew he had hit a bull's eye. He struck while the iron was hot. "Helen, I've been thinking about the time errors occurring on our journeys into and out of the rethe!" and with that he told her of his ruminations of the previous night.

She looked at him and murmured "I tell you this in the strictest confidence. This must not be revealed to any one else including Eric or Kingdom or the Prof or Judder or any one. Do you understand?"

He smiled and nodded.

She outlined to him that she herself and the Whistler were struggling to find a way to study these issues without even a whisper of their work getting out. "We are struggling to find a decent name for it!" she added.

"In all conscience you must involve the top spacemen, and I should think that the Prof or Judder could well come up with a decent name for the project!" he replied.

Her facial expression was of an approving style and he smiled again saying "Gotcha!"

"Oh all right, all right, I will put that to the Whistler later today!"

CHAPTER 3

THE PROJECT GETS UNDER WEIGH

Helen met James on the cark park on the way in again.

"Good morning Helen, before we get in I must say that I want the top spacemen, the Prof and Judder in on our little secret!"

"So there's no use me saying that I promised Henrik that I would ask for the top spacemen, the Prof and Judder to be in on it then?"

The Whistler beamed. "It's good to start off on the right foot! Have you had any further thoughts, because I have a suspicion that everything is tied up with the reorientation factor in the rethe. You remember when Captain Johnson instinctively turned his ship the full 180 before trying to exit the rethe, neither he nor the Prof noticed that without experiencing any feelings of acceleration, the ship was still heading for its target and was the right way round when they did exit the rethe. When three ships went in together with FB1, they all came out still on course in spite of the manoeuvres carried out in the rethe."

"Well it looks like another party at the Prof's place to me!"

"Hmmmm, I suppose that is a good way to get every one together without raising eyebrows. I've got almost a fortnight of untaken holiday to have, what is your position?"

"Three weeks!" she mumbled through the biscuit as she slurped her coffee, but we can't both be away for that time!"

"Ok, you get yourself and Henrik over to the Prof's place and discuss things for let's say three days, say Wednesday, Thursday and Friday. I will come over on Friday evening and I will stay for about another five days, but you could be back on the Monday so we have adequate cover here. That way we could enjoy the Prof's company for longer than usual, and you could get Judder over there for the week end, and I'll get Eric and Kingdom to come over on the Sunday afternoon provided their calendars agree. Every interested party can put their two pennyworth in, and depending on what comes up I can let you know what is going on!"

She nodded her assent as they went into the lift then along to her office for their usual Monday morning brew up.

The Whistler stood in the centre of the office and rang the Prof. The Prof answered almost immediately, and his slightly shimmering image was in the holographic cabinet as he spoke. "Can't manage without me then?" he grinned.

Liz suddenly plumped into view as she entered the Prof's holograph cabinet's transmitter camera angle and smiled as she saw who the Prof was chatting to.

"Erm Prof, I wonder if we could come over for a few days to chat things over starting say a week on Monday?"

Liz spoke up "yep, that should be fine; I've still got a few things to do down in Gloucester, but that should be largely done by then!"

"I see she's keeping you in line then" cracked the Whistler, "I'll be in touch in a few days so I'll speak to you soon—bye!"

After the link was broken and the images had faded, Helen grinned and said "you will never meet two more charming and polite people in your life, but they both have streaks of steel in them. I wouldn't like to upset either of them not only because it would be a petty thing to contemplate but I would fear for myself if I did!"

"Agreed!" said the Whistler, "but you can see why your dad chose the Prof as his second in command. He doesn't relish the top job so he is not ambitious for that, but he does drool over the top problems so he can get that unusual mind of his on the go. I will never have the Prof's intuitive perception it simply isn't in me, but I count myself as fortunate that I spotted the link between him and Judder. I really had to pull rank to get the research guys to fish all of that information out of the files during that party, but I am so glad that I did!"

Helen couldn't help herself with her next question, "James what happened to your wife?"

"Simple pneumonia" he replied as he stared out of a window for a while.

"Don't you want another lady friend?" Helen pursued.

He chuckled "yes I would like one, but who on earth would ever put up with the weird hours that my job entails?"

"Henrik puts up with mine and I put up with his!" she smiled. Just at that time the weekly cleaning lady knocked and entered with buckets and mops.

Helen recognised her but from where? Helen was resolute in her quest to keep her mouth closed during planned operations but in this instance, there were no such strictures.

"I recognise you, but I'm devilled if I can remember where from" she said.

The woman turned and grinned and said "I recognised you the first instance I saw you!"

Helens mind was racing, now with voice and face she physically started.

"You were the lady who told the undercrew that it was obvious that I had Captain Johnson's blood running in my veins! I never had chance to thank you for that because that little observation broke any hostility that was still in the air. I must tell you that even Captain Johnson didn't recognise that when I was first introduced to him!"

Josie Langan slowly stood up from her task, she grinned "so I'm cleverer than the Captain!" she tittered away for the next five minutes on and off.

The Whistler had watched this little exchange with an amused expression on his face. Josie Langan turned looked at the Whistler and said "well what are you staring at then?"

He smoothly went into a chat up routine, saying "well perhaps you are not the most beautiful woman in the world but you can be no lower than third and I was wondering why you are working in such a capacity when your talents obviously stretch much further?"

"You really don't want to know that but shall we say it is just a job to allow me to survive during the early years of the reformation."

"I am universally known as the Whistler, you may have heard of me…" she interrupted, "I know who you are James! Perhaps you should get on your computor and check me out!"

She was a direct lady and in her entire life had never been a wallflower type at all, but even she was surprised by his response.

"Pick you up at seven thirty this evening?"

She pinked slightly and agreed to the date, finished her routine and left the office flashing him a glowing smile.

Helen had already opened Josie's personnel file and was halfway though reading it, when the Whistler stood up and bade goodbye to Helen saying "she's going in the right direction to do my office next, see you later Helen." He departed grinning.

Helen sat there and wondered whether Josie Langan had got this cleaning job as a means to an end. She was very direct and she was not in awe of the Whistler in spite of his elevated position. James Whistler had leapt in at an uncharacteristically rapid speed. Perhaps it was Helens probing that had fired him up and boy oh boy he did not let the grass grow under his feet.

"Right then" thought Helen, "You James are going to undergo a real grilling tomorrow!" with that she simply put the episode aside and got on with the tasks in hand.

It was no surprise to Helen that there was an extra guest at the Prof's house during the next party.

CHAPTER 4

THE NEXT PARTY AT THE PROF'S.

Liz had settled into life as the Prof's wife in such a manner as to have become virtually indispensible. She enjoyed his company enormously, but these parties were the new highlight of her life. It was her that opened the door to welcome the guests in. Again the children had been sent on a venture so as to leave the adults free, and as soon as the second glass of Martian elixir was halfway gone the newness of the arrival of Josie had all but disappeared.

The Prof stared at Josie, apologised but continued to stare. He sniffed a sudden breath through his nose and said "Got it. I remember you from the canteen area on one of the big ships, and you always looked like you were about to say something but you never said it!"

"You've got half of it Prof. If you could cast your mind back you may remember that James Whistler was always at your table at the time, and I wanted to speak to him. But being only a member of the undercrew I didn't dare to speak out!"

Josie looked across and saw Helen grinning widely and chuckling with pleasure.

"It crossed my mind the other day that the cleaning job was a means to an end!" Helen said.

"The Space admin block is so secret it took me months of research to find out whereabouts James Whistler worked, and then another three months before the vacancy came up, then lo and behold on my first morning, there he was in your office and all my fears shrivelled away and within seconds he had asked me out!"

"He was very tight lipped about it all the next day. I tried every trick in the book to get him to give me some detail, but I got hardly a thing from him!"

"The bald truth is that I have loved him from the moment I first saw him, and I hope he will fall for me one day, in the meantime I am content to tag along as I am. The cleaning job will do, as it isn't that bad a job, the pay is ok and I will get to see him more often. Josie smiled and then added "is it really true that Captain Johnson didn't recognise you at first?"

"I am ashamed to say that it is!" interrupted Captain Johnson. "Josie, if I may call you that, we do owe you a debt. That remark of yours quelled quite a bit if the old resentment that was simmering, and pretty well every one realised the truth of what you were saying. I have viewed the video of that incident a time or two, so I am pleased to get the chance to thank you for helping establish the safety of my daughter."

Josie relaxed and smiled a smile of genuine pleasure. "I have never been a god fearing sort of person but the mule was just so evil, and even with his cleverness, he was noticeably evil. Perhaps I believe in the devil!" she muttered.

A protective arm encircled her waist as James Whistler appeared behind her.

"Chatting up the Captain isn't permitted you know, especially when you already have a man that loves you as I do!"

Josie heard this declaration and had to fight the tears of pleasure that threatened to engulf her, her voice though was uneven with the next words that she spoke, but she soon recovered and said "where are these runner beans, then?"

The Prof chuckled and commented "with all the mad things that I have done I am doomed to go down in history as a runner bean freak!"

Josie informed him "down in the lower levels of the undercrew there isn't a person in the Space service that doesn't know about your beans. They may be a bit sketchy on other things attributed to you but the runner beans are the tops. If I ever go back into the undercrew and say that I have actually eaten some of them, particularly at your house, I will be a celebrity!"

Liz, who was listening to all this said "Well I'll be damned!"

"Josie, did you know some of my beans are successfully growing on Stellar 2?" the Prof smiled as he realised that Josie had not known that.

A bell rang and Liz piped up "take your seats in the dining room everyone!"

The Prof enjoyed leaving the hard work of serving up his party meals to a catering company, and then he could relax. In this instance he had cooked the potatoes, runner beans and big joint of beef himself before handing over the reins.

Just at that moment two latecomers arrived and Liz welcomed the Jacksons in.

Having just got seated Hannah Jackson said "About now ladies!"

"What a swell party this is!" they chorused, even Josie Langan managed to join in the last two words.

"That I suppose is the key to this party?" she questioned, and watched as the other girls all nodded.

The dinner was served and Josie Langan nodded her approval at the Prof. It went quiet as the guests all munched their way through the meal.

The reverend Jackson spoke as he found "I know several black folk who are superb cooks, but this meal is the equal of any of them. I never knew roast beef could be so tasty!

The Prof declared "I am an Englishman, a Limey, a Gringo, a Pomme, or a Sassenach, according to which part of the world you come from, but now you know why the French call us 'les Rosbif'", and he grinned with pure delight as he knew his latest offering went down at least as well as those that had gone before. "Perhaps the Mule and the Donkey did not have enough roast beef in their diets and thus were doomed to failure!"

Liz added "if you believe that then you are top of the gullibility tree!"

So far not a word of the real reason for the party had been spoken and as it turned out, that did not happen until the following day. The party rolled on as each of the guests had small anecdotes to cough up. As it quietened down, Josie Langan managed to find a quiet corner with James Whistler. "Erm, James, I know this may be painful, and I won't dwell on it, but what happened to your wife?"

James sighed and said "time has been a good healer but my wife, daughter-in-law and my son died as a result of a road accident quite some while ago, and a tyre blowout was the reason. The death certificate did say pneumonia but it was all due to the accident in my view. Fortunately my grandson was not in the vehicle with them, and so it was left to me to help organise his upbringing. I wasn't available in the early years due to work pressures so he was fostered out, but after that during his teens I influenced him somewhat. I and all my family are what are referred to as 'intellectuals', but Eric though highly intelligent had something else. He was also a sporting type and most of his scrapes as a lad involved cuts and bruises one way or another.

I was hardened by my experiences but suddenly I acquired the nickname of 'the Weasel' a name I abhorred. Catherine and her Grandad started to refer to me in their book as the Whistler, and somehow or other even before the book was published, weasel dropped away and I became the Whistler. A bit like some character out of 'Batman' I suppose. Time has flown by and I regarded myself as too old to go looking for a girlfriend so I jumped at my only chance when it came!"

"James, it is obvious that you have a few miles on the clock, but I have seen men only in their twenties who have already become set in their ways and are effectively old before their time. I see no such problem with you--- at all!"

"Normally my blood pressure is rather on the low side, I wonder what it is just now?" there was a short silence, then he said "I have asked the Prof to provide you with a room on the right hand end of the landing if that is all right? So when you have had enough I will show you where it is."

Half an hour later he did just that, and showed her round the rest of the Prof's house first. His mouth ran a little dry as he closed the bed room door behind him.

"Well where is your room? She asked archly.

"I don't have one!" he admitted.

"I told you that you had no signs of aging, and I see that I am totally correct!"

He put the light out.

Downstairs, the party had begun to wind down, and the Jacksons were the first to leave, and they went home. The others all had business the following day and one by one they retired to their allotted rooms. The Prof and Liz were the last to remain downstairs, and Liz asked the Prof what the business was during the following few days.

For once in his life the Prof didn't really know. He smiled at Liz and said "well we will see tomorrow, but I think they are puzzled by certain unaccounted time slips during their later voyages."

"Is our house going to host a forum on the most advanced scientific issues?" asked Liz. Liz felt chuffed as the Prof nodded in the affirmative. They decided to retire soon after and stood aside as the caterers expertly gathered the trash up and cleaned the rooms before making their swift exit.

"Well even if they had made a hash of the evening, which they didn't, the caterers shear energy and speed in cleaning up was recommendation in itself. All in all I think they did a good job, but from here on in, we are on our own!" the Prof smiled warmly at Liz and she smiled back as they wearily climbed the stairs. Mind you they weren't quite as weary as they believed.

CHAPTER 5

THE BUSINESS SIDE GETS GOING

Bacon sandwiches were offered for breakfast; the Prof had got the caterers to grill the bacon up during the previous evening and used the microwave to warm things up.

Jane Johnson asked Josie what her family history entailed. Josie spoke up saying she was the youngest of five. She had been married and followed the traditional things in life until her husband ran off with another woman.

"That did shock me" she admitted, "and I basically ran away and joined the Space service. I am quite hardy really and once I got over the blow to my pride I set about doing my job well. The arrival of the mule was a problem, because the earth's politicians had made it so easy for him, a large proportion of the undercrew were persuaded to give him his chance. I admit that I was in sympathy with some of the things that he said, but I had lost my parents a few months before and so he never had the 'loved ones' hold over me that he had over others. Most folk realised too late just what a duplicitous liar the mule was and by then he had a firm grip on the reins of power, and I didn't exactly despair, but I was not a happy bunny. One day we all had to attend the great hall and when we were assembled there I was right at the front. Helen Johnson appeared on the dais and I was struck immediately by her resemblance to Captain Johnson without even knowing who she was. One aggressive man, I forget his name just now, interrupted her as she was explaining what the meeting was about and he rushed towards the dais she was standing on. She called out for the man to be restrained but we were all too shocked to move, so she smoothly took a firearm from a holster behind her back, slipped off the safety catch and calmly shot him in the leg. He did swear! I didn't need any more proof. There was still some simmering discontent, but I bawled out words to the effect that was everybody blind because it was obvious to me that she had Captain Johnson's blood running in her veins."

Jane replied "she glossed over that assault bit when she told me about it; that must have been a scary moment!"

"It was shortly after that that I saw the Whistler as he is universally known, in the canteen, and although he is a good bit older than me, I found I couldn't get him out of my head. I went to some lengths to try and find when he would next be there but I never got to speak to him. Then the Donkey intervened and I along with many others lost my job. With him gone, Helen got the pay system up and running and I jumped at the first chance of a job in the Space centre. The rest of it you know!"

Jane smiled and said "I regard Helen almost as a sister not a step daughter so she can expect some stick from me. Fancy not telling me just how close she was to a serious assault!"

Helen joined them at the breakfast table just then and was mystified by the imperious beckoning forefinger on Jane's left hand.

"Ah yes" she agreed as she was informed of Jane's beef, "I did go a bit light on detail on that, but when I told you about it I had only known you about half an hour and I didn't want to risk anything that might bring you or dad some problems! After all I was a big enough problem for you to swallow on my own."

"Catherine Whistler had shown me archive records so I knew all about you, and the fact that the Cap didn't even know about you himself!"

"Oooh, now I remember, it was your voice that ordered me to come in! I tell you I was terrified. I had really missed having a dad, and had only just got one so I knew my whole happiness was tied up in how you saw me. I was so choked up when I saw your genuine smile I remember us both having a tearful moment!"

"You, me and the Cap, we owe one to Catherine Whistler. Without her I would have had no foreknowledge, and I might have hated you on sight."

"Truly I hope you wouldn't have hated me. The first I saw you I knew we could be friends, so no more secrets. Right!"

Mouths were filled with bacon and the only other incident at breakfast was when Josie Langan dissolved into tears for a few seconds. "Because I am so happy" she wailed.

After breakfast the men and Helen went into the Prof's sitting room and the complexities of their problems were examined point by point. After the first hour or so the Whistler, drew breath and summarised.

"Gentlemen I will re-state what we have talked of this morning. It all starts with what we know or have observed.

Right at the outset Helen's notion that the rethe seems to possess zero time has been borne out. The only time that is involved is the amount spent inside our ether cocoon. Again, credit for realising that this time element while spent inside the world of anti-matter is inverted; goes to Helen. We know from Henrik's spec of dust decimal point that the figures seem to hold true. That may have caused us some wasted time in Space but it served to prove Helen's point, confirming the truth of her theory.

While exploring the Stellar two region we let FB1 out. Was this a coincidence that after our close encounter with it we seem to have locked ourselves away for the best part of three years? When fetching FB1 back to our own galaxy, we seemed to not have lost, and possibly may have gained some time.

I went with Doctor Barry and studied FB1 and Sonny, I was in close proximity and I circled round both of them and so far as I know I did not loose or gain any time. The reason for my studies was to show that there is a small volume in each fireball where there is a constant exchange between the ether and the rethe and as molecules from each side meet; a lot of heat is given off, as anti- matter and real matter collide and fuse, thus disappearing. It seems that we take a cocoon of ether into the rethe with us so its stands to reason that there must be a similar thing the other way round. FB1 and Sonny each has a negative cocoon but it is punctured thus permitting the two way flow all the time. Does this produce neutrons? Are we on the brink of finding out what a neutron star really is and are we nearer to explaining the actions of a black hole? Inside an atom the whole world knows we have protons electrons and neutrons, but just where do neutrons come from and how is it that they don't acquire an electric charge like a proton? Do Sonny and FB1 fuse negative and positive components to produce neutrons? The scientific physicists have investigated the forces at work within the atom, and they are now very advanced, and yet I think there is truly another dimension to the issue, and we in the Space service, specialists in our own field, may uncover something vital.

Henrik here has posed a good question and one that we can act on directly. He has asked what if two ships enter the rethe in synchronism but through different black portals, both headed for the same target but with a different time element so that one came out of the rethe at day one where the other came out at day three, for sake of argument. Would the ships be visible to each other, and what would their on board timing systems reveal?

If they were stationary at the target space co-ordinates would the second ship become visible to the first ship after three days or what? If the ships were moving would the two never meet, or would they appear as a ghost or what? Are things any different from two ships heading out to the same co-ordinates simply three days apart?

Whenever ships have entered the rethe, they have always exited on the same heading irrespective of movements inside our cocoons, we have relied on this yet we have no explanation for it.

I have always prided myself on being a reasoned individual. Rashness is not in my nature, and yet I find that I have contributed to space ventures, have participated in them myself, when now it appears that we have virtually no knowledge of what we were doing and only by some dint of extreme good fortune or some hidden laws of physics are we all here to discuss the matter.

Gentlemen and lady, we have some serious work to do." He sat down to a deafening round of silence, as the delegates pondered his words.

A door opened and the ladies joined them with a steaming brew of tea.

Judder spoke up. "I think the only contribution that I can make is to think of a name for the project, so I'll concentrate on that and leave you other guys to worry about the many dire consequences that we all face."

The delegates sat down and each man thought of what had been mentioned as he sipped his tea.

"Sugar if any body wants it!" said Liz, glancing at the Prof as she spoke. The Prof was away with the fairies just then so Liz smiled to herself and at Helen and gracefully left the room.

Sipping of tea was the only noise to be heard over the next twenty minutes, but there were some deeply furrowed brows.

In spite of his promise to confine himself to a name for the project Judder suddenly spoke out. "Why don't we do what Henrik suggested and send two ships out to check on what happens and then perhaps we will have some of the down clues as well as the cross ones!"

Helen and the Whistler both smiled at Judder's use of the crossword as an analogy of their problems, but inwardly they knew he was right.

The Whistler said "ok I think we should do that but in the meantime let us consider each of the issues I thought up right at the beginning. If I can remember them all."

A voice from the back of the room piped up, "I have everything typed onto my computor, if that is of any use. No-one had noticed Catherine Whistler at the back, but James Whistler was delighted that she had found a way to make a real contribution. Catherine hit the print function and the Prof's printer whirred as it spewed out a copy for everyone.

"It is unedited so I accept no criticism on spelling" warned Catherine with her usual cheeky grin, "But I'll take a cup of that tea and a biscuit." Across in the breakfast room the printer in there whirred and Jane Johnson picked up the print out and read its contents with fascination.

Judder whooped "Space condensation in the rethe to be studied more deeply on a health and safety basis."

Helen added "That will do. It tells the truth. But it is vague enough to permit us to do almost anything."

Judder spoke up again "Is it safe to use the jump still. Or do we wait for the various points under discussion to be resolved, what do we tell the outside world?"

Captain Johnson intervened saying "I see no reason to avoid using the jump unless we have to. Fortunately only the Moneybag has had to do a jump regularly, all journeys to mars are done using mark 2 gravity motor control and so there is no point in engendering panic. Or do you think otherwise James?"

James Whistler put his hands behind his head and drew several deep breaths. "A few days ago I would have had no reason to fret about Space travel using the jump. Just now though, things are different. From the standpoint of pure logic, there is no known reason to interfere with commercial Space flights. In our case I trust ignorance truly is bliss. We have a number of conundrums to look at. At the end of the day many of our fears could be groundless, yet instinct warns me to be careful. I will put it to the board that we are slowly giving more credibility to 'Space condensation in the rethe' as we strive to ensure that commercial flights don't run into any unexplained and dangerous phenomena.

The costs of Space flight are enormous, but thanks to the diamond shards from Triton are more than sustainable without our organisation going to governments with our begging bowl."

The Prof came out of his deep thinking mode and quietly asked if an alloying experiment could be carried out. The alloy of lead and aluminium made during early flights to the delight of metallurgists, turned out to be of little value. The resulting metal had a low melting point, wasn't very strong or springy but was quite heavy, with decent corrosion resistance. There was work ongoing in the motor industry to examine the properties of this alloy with a view to using it for crankshaft bearings but so far the alloy was proving of little value.

The Prof asked if a bar of lead and a similar sized bar of aluminium could be carried, one on each ship but going into the rethe at the same time and exiting three days apart. Each bar would be manually placed at a known co-ordinate position and then its positioner would wait as the three days expired to see what would happen.

"The bar could become a composite, or would remain two separate entities, either way some insight into the behaviour would be gained."

Judder said "Nice one dad, we could place them in orbit round Mars or Venus retire some distance away and see what happens, or it could be done as part of some other mission, just to save costs. Thinking about it, the Moneybag enters the rethe through the black portal near Venus so it would only be a few hours diversion and the jump time could be adjusted to restore the ship to its expected schedule! The Moneybag could collect the result on the way back."

"I think Doctor Barry is due a stint on the Moneybag starting next week, and we could inform him of our reasons so the Captain wouldn't be in the dark so to speak. It sounds like a goer to me!" Eric Whistler spoke with his customary enthusiasm.

The Whistler and Captain Johnson both grinned at the mention of the Captain "not being in the dark" but nothing was said.

Captain Johnson spoke up again. "Neither I nor the Prof noticed the heading issue when we first exited the rethe. Now I admit there were other very pressing matters to consider, but we have now had other similar issues like when we brought FB1 to the Solar system. There was considerable movement inside our cocoon yet the ships and the fireball all exited exactly as we entered. One would expect the sensation of violent angular acceleration to be felt as the ships were spun back onto their original course. My conclusion based on the fact that no such forces were felt, is that any movement in the rethe is not real, it is only apparent. The rethe must have some quality to permit this."

Judder's face was animated. "Kingdom Johnson has to be correct. Therefore once in the rethe I think that we must have been inside subsidiary cocoons. As we re-orientated our selves, our own cocoon simply moved equal and opposite, but somehow twisted our visual perception so that we thought we had carried out our moves. If you think about it, as I understand things once in the rethe you are at your destination immediately and only from within the cocoon does any time element appear. The rethe thus destroys accelerational concepts because that involves time. So it equally must destroy any relative motional or distance concepts because they also involve time. Suck on that for a bit!"

Captain Johnson hearing his name spoken again realised that gradually more and more people were using his name and much to his surprise, he was finding that he really didn't mind at all.

Helen suddenly excitedly squeaked "the light waves giving us visual perception are undergoing several total internal reflections so that our wriggling around in the rethe did permit us to bring the incoming heat from fireball onto our heat shields, and protect ourselves. It all fits."

Mr. Robot face suddenly rose from his reverie. "We are definitely on the right track here, and my fears for using the jump are receding. We must however issue a new directive regarding the ether time element calculation and put it at Captain Johnson's figures plus or minus say five percent. That can also be put to the board. I will say that we are urgently looking into that but in the meantime all commercial flights are to stick to the figure at present in use until we authorise differently. He smiled and his face relaxed.

Catherine was still typing furiously over in the corner as they all broke for a break.

Outside munching on a beef sandwich prepared by Liz, the Prof was proud of Brian. "I really think he has put his finger on that issue. When you analyse the problems there were only two. The first was the heading problem and this is the first explanation of this. I believe it will be correct. Possibly James and Helen may find the idea needs tidying up a little due to their deliberations in the maths required, but the fundamentals are in place. The other issue is to square away all of the time errors, and I believe that will of necessity need more Space trips, and possibly many of them."

Judder heard the Prof say that and commented "when I went in there today I just didn't think I had any chance of making a positive contribution because I don't have the brains or the education, but I did ok didn't I?"

Nadine, who had been quieter than usual came across, with two plates of sandwiches. "Get this down you before your brain seizes up! she ordered. "You know Prof, even before I knew he was your son, I always had faith in him. He just suddenly fires on an extra cylinder and you have to be quick to keep up with him!"

"Hello Nadine" smiled the Prof, "I'm not ignoring you but quite honestly the problem that Brian has just offered an enlightening opinion on has been so difficult to grasp that I have been with Alice in Wonderland for the last two days. Come and sit here and bring me up to date with family news!"

The Prof listened avidly while she regaled him with her children's adventures and their knocks and bruises. This had until recently been missing from the Prof's life and he drank the details greedily and happily.

Just then there was a knock on the front door, the Prof went to open it but Liz got there first.

It was a parcel delivery service asking for a signature. The address was unusual it said

Runner beans from Stellar 2.

To the Prof.

Earth.

"How did they get the beans back to earth unless they used their shuttle? It does have jump capability" mused the Prof, and he wondered whether there was anything sinister about the parcel. He alerted the others and they all went into the Prof's greenhouse while he opened the packet. There was a letter inside and the Prof said "you've got to hand it to the mail boys. They have delivered me a parcel from outer space. I suppose it must mean that I'm famous!" he read it out loud:

'Dear Prof we had to use our brains to get this package back to the Solar system, so we hope it arrives undamaged and finds you. Sorry about the address but it was all that we know of you. The original beans left by Captain Johnson have been prolific, and we have grown quite a few new plants that were progeny of the originals. If you plant these they will grow and produce more beans but they will be bright green in colour if they are anything like ours up here. These have almost supplanted potatoes as our staple diet, but we have competition because the chickens like them even more than they like the local seaweed.

Captain Johnson warned us that we might suffer premature ageing but so far as we are quite young, we have seen absolutely no sign of it. Captain Johnson also mentioned that we may find an advantage as this planet is still virgin with regards to the existence of life. He could well be right because since we have been eating the local strain of the beans no-one has had a cold lasting more than about four hours, and we are-touch wood- all in robust health.

Yours, on behalf of all the stellar 2 wallahs, Jack Robinson.'

PS, we have had nine more children! We are able now to get about without using any oxygen supplements. We still get out of breath more easily than on earth but we are I am sure adapting to our environment.

The Prof grinned "my cup runneth over! Next spring I shall be tending Martian mushrooms and Stellar two beans. Oh happy days!"

Note from Catherine Whistler: It looks like another visit to Stellar 2 is on the cards.

During the next few days the various folk still at the party went about their business and were homeward bound generally as the Whistler's plan. When the Whistler himself next showed up for work a very curious Helen Svensson was waiting for him.

CHAPTER 6

JANE JOHNSON HAS A THINK ABOUT THINGS

Jane had been devoted to family life for some time now, but her curious mind was still whirling her thoughts around.

Back at home she read the printout again and again and finally she broached the subject with her husband.

"Cap!" she called and got no response "Kingdom!" she yelled out. This time he raised his head and smiled, "yes, squirt, what can I do for you?"

She spoke to him of the alloying issue using a time jump. "Well you know about this idea of sending two ships on the same co-ordinates with different rethe time? Well I thought it might be better to introduce another time element in. What I am thinking is that each of the metal bars must have a magnet in it so that they will try to attract each other, just in case there is a slight positional error when the constituent parts are placed at their target positions. I also think a video camera must be set running in the vicinity.

I further think that the first ship should exit the rethe at day one and place its load at the target position. That ship must then return to the start position making a jump to get there. The second ship must start off heading for the same target position but must deposit its load on day two. This ship must immediately return to the start position using the jump.

Both ships must then enter the rethe together but aim to exit at a different portal, and exit on day three. They can then search for the camera and fused metal bars if they are to be found, and bring all of the data back for analysis. This way if there should be a cataclysm, our ships should be well away from it at the time. I know it is long winded but we have lost no-one yet and I don't want to lose my best friends."

Kingdom Johnson thought deeply about what she had said and could understand her motives for saying what she said. It was sound logic. He had been about to call the Whistler as she spoke up and he used his mobile phone to record what she was saying. He pressed the buttons on his phone and sent the recorded message as a voicemail to the Whistler.

The Whistler was out, but Helen was at her desk and she routinely went through the Whistler's incoming mail. She listened to Jane's voice and could not fault the logic, and in fact she knew that James Whistler would approve. The idea would satisfy his innate desire for safety.

She sent a voice mail back thanking Jane and saying she would draw the Whistler's attention to it immediately. She then forwarded the message on to James who was spending some time with the board.

The board had hawks and doves, and keeping the excessive aggression of the hawks in check was becoming increasingly difficult.

James had had enough.

"Right ho you bloodthirsty types. If you want to put you money where your mouth is you can accompany me on the next mission. I will warn you however that your constituent atoms could be spread over the galaxy as a result of your uninformed and pathetic impatience. The loss of a ship and some eighteen thousand crew would set the Space service back a thousand years, but if it gets rid of you it may well be worth it!"

Just at that moment his mobile throbbed in his pocket. As he was waiting a reaction from the board, he read through Jane's idea, and was struck at once by the idea of keeping the spaceships away from the collision moment in time, and it gave him another pole to his argument. There was still no response from the board members.

"Chew on this if you like! I have just received a message from the wife of Captain Johnson. She was the first person ever to see and record extra terrestrial life, so she has been round the block.

He outlined her idea to them and gave them a few seconds thinking time.

"Now we can proceed as she says or we could proceed as some of you would have me do, with singletons taking massive risks; we will ask for a volunteer crew to take you hawks and you can go at your desired breakneck speed. I will follow the plan outlined by Jane Johnson and I will endeavour to collect the remnants of your ship and you lot if I can."

"You are exaggerating!" came a voice from the far end of the table.

James Whistler smiled grimly, "I cannot exaggerate because I do not know what will happen, however I think attempting avoidance of total disaster is best. All those with me vote now." All hands went up except one.

"I will do nothing at all unless I get a unanimous vote, other than try to remove you from this board!" the Whistler threatened.

There was still no movement from the remaining hawk.

"As of this moment none of you has any experience of Space travel, so I must call an extraordinary shareholders meeting, where the motion will be that 'only those with experience of interstellar travel will be permitted to sit on this board', and I know I will have a lot of sympathisers with that view."

The final hand went up as accepting the proposal put forward, but the Whistler was not finished.

"I will not call an extraordinary meeting but I intend to put that motion at the AGM, so you can all think on that!"

Of the seven other members, four immediately requested to be considered for the next Space mission. Three were doves and only one was a hawk.

James Whistler gracefully accepted the volunteers, and then added, "You may not be aware of this but I fought with the resistance during the upheavals, and I really had hoped that that alone would have rid me of the dreadful nickname of "THE WEASEL!" He was angry now. "It would appear that some of you still really think of me as such a character. You will find that I am not weak or sneaky at all. I know that only one of you fought with the resistance. Others have simply come out of the woodwork as soon as the fighting was all over. You may think that this has gone un-noticed. It has not. Many folk had their wealth confiscated by the Donkey. Now we are well into the reformation, great efforts have been made by those folk to reclaim what they see as their rightful place with its attendant privileges, and they are failing in that mostly because their wealth was dissipated by the Donkey and his cohorts.

If any of you think that you have the right to ask this organisation to send thousands of men to their deaths by precipitate actions you are wrong. If you can not square your consciences with the way the Space administration behaves I will have your resignations now!"

Two angry men stood up to leave. "You will be deemed to have resigned the moment you are through that door!"

"You can't speak to us like that!" spat out one of the two standing.

"I can, I will, I have, and I am fully justified in so doing. Your attitude is a disgrace, and I will have your signed resignations now!" roared the Whistler. He got them.

After the departing directors had gone James turned to the shorthand secretary and asked if she had got it all down. "Every word" said his PA. She had known James Whistler for many years now and had been surprised that he could find so much venom. "Weasel never, tough cookie, definitely" she thought to herself.

The hawk that had precipitated all this was still sat at the end of the table and he now spoke. "James, I stand corrected. When a man with that amount of fire in his belly urges caution we must all listen. Unfortunately this means I shall have to add my name to the list of Space flight volunteers! I suppose you must realise that I was expressing ideas that were partly my own but were stoked up by our late brethren. I must say I was surprised at how quickly they capitulated and would not fight for the ideas they so cunningly fostered in me. I will not be taken in like that again."

James Whistler relaxed. "Ok, thank you for your forbearance gentlemen. I will not select you for any missions with perceived danger. As we proceed during this time of unprecedented Space exploration every little anomaly must be studied carefully. I expect some answers to come quickly whilst others may take years to emerge, but answers must be found. It is our bounden duty to find answers. As you may imagine those at the very forefront of space travel can uncover problems at an alarming rate. This I know from direct experience. The captains of these missions must have full field commander power to do what is perceived to be necessary without having the spectre of dismissal hanging over them if a mistake is made, and they must have the power to refuse a perceived stupid instruction from earth. We are studying certain time anomalies at the moment and we have laid down strictures for commercial flights using the jump. If those parameters are adhered to there is no indication that undue danger will present itself.

Exploration flights are a different kettle of fish and that is why my proposals have been outlined a few minutes ago. Now may I trouble you for another show of hands please? For the motion ah! Unanimous, that's what I like to see!"

He brought the meeting to a close and decided right there and then that a vice chairman was required and the erstwhile hawk would be his choice in the matter.

Chatting to Helen he told her that he had full backing for the Space exploration and time anomaly resolutions. She raised her eyebrows as he and gave her a disc saying "My PA took shorthand notes, but they will not show the drama, view this disc!"

Helen viewed the disc, and said "I would love to show a copy of that to my dad!

You fought like a heavyweight boxer with lead-lined gloves, but I think the original hawk actually looks like he could be a good man!"

"He hasn't received my e-mail yet because I am still editing it, but I am going to offer him the post of vice chairman. He can officiate when I am not available! And if you wait twenty four hours you can show that disc to your dad and to Henrik if you like."

When Kingdom Johnson viewed it he shook his head almost disbelievingly. "James Whistler would be the last man to indulge in fisticuffs, but he stood up to be counted there and no mistake. I always felt there was an undercurrent of power to the man. Josie Langan will be bursting with pride I think. No matter what our trials and tribulations are when we are away, it is a prerequisite to know that someone with some spine is in your corner, back home."

He sent the Whistler a text message that simply said "OUCH!"

CHAPTER 7

SOME POSITIVE ACTION AT LAST

The Whistler thought long and hard about the composition of the next mission. He decided that on cost grounds shuttles would be the favourite vessels for the job; also the human cost would be more bearable if the unthinkable happened.

Shuttles were big enough to carry rations for several weeks and had the capacity to get up to warp 0.99 and thus could make the jump.

The Whistler asked for volunteers and was gratified to find at least twice as many as he needed. He put the names in a hat and asked Helen to pull out three names. Helen found that this took more courage than she had anticipated but in the end none of the senior Space Captains were in the selection.

The mission was quite simple. Ship one would make the jump and exit the rethe five days later. Ship two would enter the rethe and exit it three days later and ship three would enter the rethe and reappear after only one day. The exit point was chosen as a blue portal on the outer extremities of the asteroid belt. Ship three would leave a bar of zinc into which was cast a powerful permanent magnet. It would have a red end that was to be left pointing at the sun. A camera would be left in the vicinity, recording events. Ship three would then make a second jump and exit the rethe near to Jupiter, in the asteroid belt.

Ship two would exit and then proceed to the destination and would leave an aluminium bar again but with a blue magnetic end which was to be left pointing at the sun. The reason for the painted ends was to ensure that the magnets would attract and not repel each other. Ship two would also leave a camera in the vicinity and would leave it running.

Ship two would then make the jump to the Jupiter area and await events as they unfolded.

Ship one would exit the rethe and proceed to the rendezvous, and then report on findings.

The all important ship was the number one vessel, but nobody knew what the number two vessel would experience.

Doctor Barry would head the number one ship, Judder would head the number two ship and Heinrich would head the number three ship.

In the event Heinrich's part of the mission went without a problem, but Judder's ship saw previously unseen activities.

As Judder manoeuvred his shuttle to the given co-ordinates he felt the reduced amount of control function. This was not expected and Judder's crew recorded the data accurately. As they neared the meeting point the crew viewed what seemed to be a translucent bar and a camera. Judder used his experience and had the crew carry out old fashioned film camera photographs as well as modern digital ones. He placed his bar at the exact co-ordinate and then slowly withdrew observing as he went. He left his own video camera filming the reaction. He observed the strange phenomenon of watching the solid bar and the translucent bar trying to conjoin, and as he drew further away he noticed that the two bars were writhing and began to glow. The magnets held the ends of the bars together but the centres seemed to bend with the softness of plastiscene. He reluctantly headed for his portal and made the jump as planned.

Doctor Barry exited the rethe on schedule and went to examine the target site. He retrieved the cameras and the bars and made his jump out to the edges of the asteroid belt. All were present and correct and the mission then returned to earth with the prized data.

The Whistler asked the Prof if he would like to make a rare appearance at the space centre and offered to put him and Liz up for the night. The Prof was intrigued to say the least. On the day in question Helen went down into reception to meet the Prof and Liz, and issued them with a pass for the day, then up in the lift and along to the Whistler's office. Josie Langan was in there in her cleaner's uniform and actually looked very smart. She told Liz that she actually liked the cleaning duty because she met so many interesting people and she wasn't planning to give it up even after her forthcoming wedding.

"Forthcoming wedding? I thought Bill was a fast mover but James has excelled himself!"

"You ought to see the disc of the last board meeting if you want to get to know about James," she said. "Follow me!"

She took Liz into the coffee break area and showed her the disc and hopped along to the important bit. Liz sat with both eyebrows arched and grinned." No wonder you couldn't get him out of your head!"

Back in the Whistler's office the Prof was turning the amalgamated bar round in his hands as he looked at it.

"The bars seem to have fought against amalgamisation but the magnets seem to have done the opposite." He said thoughtfully.

"Those magnets have the most powerful attraction I have ever seen for something of that size" commented the Whistler, as he dropped a paper clip some three feet away. The clip shot across to the magnet. "I am wondering whether old Einstein was really close to an earth shattering discovery all those years ago. Judder reported that he felt the reduced controllability of his shuttle as he approached to put the second bar in place. He was nowhere near a black or a blue portal. But the magnetic forces applied by the magnets were massive as they held the bars together in spite of other massive forces trying to keep them apart. If there is a direct link between magnetism and gravity then that would account for Judder's difficulty in controlling the approach of his shuttle. If we had sent bigger ships on this mission it is possible that their shear mass would have precluded us from making this discovery. I have no answers only more questions, of course the apparent attraction from the magnets may not be entirely magnetic, and it could have a gravitational component!"

"I can smell coffee!" said the Prof.

"Only vending machine stuff, but it tastes ok" said the Whistler as they walked in and found their ladies talking.

Liz said "Bill. You had better see this!"

The Prof watched the disc and then chortled "Well that sure told them! I knew you had it in you James so I'm dead chuffed to be right again."

"He's my hero!" smiled Josie.

"All right, all right" said the Whistler, as he squirmed slightly under the praise, and he showed the Prof the text message from Captain Johnson.

The Prof chuckled and said "well in a single word, Kingdom got that spot on!"

"Now we have got that out of the way can we consider the implications of what our missions accomplished, please?"

The Prof nodded and looked at the metal bars again. As he moved the bar round in his hands he suddenly felt the attraction of his wristwatch strap to the magnet, this surprised him because the strap was stainless steel, which was supposedly non magnetic.

The Whistler placed a wooden spatula on the table and even that was attracted. The Prof's eyebrows rose and he asked "is this dia-magnetism instead of paramagnetism, or even perhaps paragravity?"

The Whistler admitted that that hadn't actually occurred to him but said "well I wonder if it isn't some sort of gravity being generated and it seems to attract stuff in proportion to its density or weight."

"Now then" he continued "Judder's camera revealed this. He hit the play button on his computor and the Prof watched as the aluminium and zinc bars writhed against each other as they tried to escape the clutches of the magnets, and finally glowed with the heat.

"The heat will be due to friction" said the Prof, "if you bend any bars of metal that much they will get hot! Amazingly the heat doesn't seem to take the magnets through their Curie point!"

The Whistler nodded and advised he had already commissioned lab tests to try to prove that and was some way to confirming it.

The Whistler replayed the early part of the disc and the Prof said "Christ they look translucent! They occupy the space but not in that time co-ordinate, perhaps that really does explain the apparitions that allegedly appear from time to time on earth."

"Yes only one of the bars was translucent when they were placed in position but now both of them appear that way, there is not one answer here but we have a whole new load of questions."

The Prof nodded and then said "I think we should pay a restocking visit to Stellar two. Keep a meticulous detail of all operations carried out and see if we can't give ourselves some more clues as to what we are dealing with here."

The Whistler agreed, promising to thank Jack Robinson for the beans sent to the Prof. In this case they would tread an already trodden path so decided to limit the mission to only two ships. Just at that point there was a knock at the door. Upon receiving an enter command the door opened and there stood our erstwhile hawk, who then came in and introduced himself.

"Good afternoon ladies and gentlemen. My name is Jarvis Kellar."

"Please come in and sit down" said the Whistler "Would you like to read this" and with that James Whistler handed over his mobile phone. Jarvis Kellar read then re-read the message, looked up and said "well I will be delighted to accept!"

Jarvis Kellar then let it be known what had brought him to James Whistler's office.

"After your Richard the Lion Heart performance yesterday, the two directors who stormed off have had time to rethink their positions, and have begged me to intercede on their behalves. I liked what I heard from you yesterday and frankly I mention this to you only because I promised I would bring up their case. If it were left to me I would not touch them with a barge pole, now I have seen what they are made of."

James Whistler grinned a delightful mischievous grin and said "that then is your first task Jarvis! You can use whatever language you like but I have many reasons for wanting rid of that pair, so go to it!------- --------- oh and don't forget to sign it as deputy chairman of the Space Administration."

Jarvis Kellar smiled a small smile and went away to compose a suitable letter.

The Prof chuckled and said "I am glad I'm retired! But I do think James that that man will be up to the mark. Cometh the hour cometh the man."

James Whistler then added "in these early days of the reformation we have to set examples so that those that follow will have a tradition to uphold. That pair of overbearing fools had wealth, and position within their organisations. Now they have to explain why they resigned, to their own boards, and without doubt we will be inundated with requests to maintain their company's representation on our board. They simply overlooked the fact that as directors of the Space administration they had no executive powers. They were here with honorary directorships and as observers to watch over their companies interests but had never been expected or empowered to run our organisation. The promised threat I made to the board that day will be acted upon. I wish to adopt the motion that only those with direct experience of interstellar travel can sit on the board. I don't think I will have any mountains to climb there but with a vice chairman to support me I hope to avoid much of the infighting. They tried to remove me once before and as they have found out; I don't cave in at the first sign."

The three women at the back of the room gave a sudden burst of spontaneous applause.

The Whistler added, "I think any organisation must have directors who know a substantial amount about what the company does. We cannot have divisive inputs from ignorant fools such as we have just moved on. They were all mouth and overbearing aggression and had not one jot of thought for our Space crews. Each ship can have almost twenty thousand souls on board and I will not abide anyone who wishes to ignore that fact!" he glanced at the ladies then grinned as he realised he had only just avoided another round of applause.

"We need to plan our next mission to Stellar 2. Should you have any ideas Prof, use the holographic TV link. By the way what do you think of the holographic reception?"

"Unbelievably real. The only thing that gives it away other than the slightly echoey sound is when some one moves off camera, they just seem to be swallowed up, and they sort of slither down an unseen slot just off the edge of the screen!"

"Ok thanks for coming across. We have a nice little meal set out in the executive canteen, and I'm sure the ladies would like that." They all trooped off to the canteen on the eighth floor. As they got there they found a patient Jarvis Kellar trying to persuade the canteen manageress to let him in. She was having none of it but the Whistler said jovially "Mrs. Wisdom, Jarvis Kellar is now as of today the deputy chairman of the Space Administration. Perhaps I should have told you first but it slipped my mind!" Mrs. Wisdom somewhat mollified looked across rather doubtfully at Josie Langan's cleaner's uniform and James continued "perhaps I can make the first introduction of my future wife. Mrs Wisdom, please meet Josie Langan and I dare say I should also introduce Mrs. Bill Wild, the Prof's new wife!"

Nancy Wisdom capitulated and smiled and mouthed sorry across to Jarvis Kellar.

Jarvis was quite a gallant sort and replied "I am glad that we are on the same side Mrs. Wisdom. I do not want to cross you and well done for standing up for your beliefs!"

"Call me Nancy" she replied smiling fully now.

The Whistler popped his laptop onto the table and after fiddling with it smiled.

Helen said "James what are you up to?"

"Just checking personnel records!" he smiled again.

"Why are you doing that?" whispered Josie.

He whispered back "I really will have to get you to re-polish your observational skills a little when we're married. There was a definite frisson between our new deputy chairman and Mrs. Wisdom. I was just checking to see if the coast is clear!"

She shook her head in wonderment saying "There can be no faster man than you on such things, how did you remain unattached for so long?"

"Search me!" he whispered then looked across at the Prof and Liz "not up to your standards I am sure, but not bad for a canteen eh?"

"Actually" said the Prof "this is one of the best canteen meals I've ever had and your staff is to be congratulated". The Whistler beckoned Mrs Wisdom, across and told her of the opinions expressed around the table. Nancy Wisdom was pleased to say the least. "Do you know who this is?" He indicated the Prof to her.

"Well he is the Prof isn't he?" she said.

"Yes he is but did you know his full title is 'Sir William Wild?'"

Nancy Wisdom fetched all of her staff out and introduced them to Sir William and Lady Elizabeth Wild.

The Prof for the first time in his life suffered the pangs of embarrassment, but he smiled graciously and Liz was muttering about updating their letter head. Her mind ran over the next party invites

"Lady Elizabeth and Sir William Wild cordially invite......" a satisfied smirk filled her face and the Prof said "steady on Liz it's only us you know!"

She knew that he had reasoned out why she was smirking and she marvelled at his uncanny ability to make such deductions so quickly. That's why everyone else called him the Prof.

As they were making their way home later that day she smiled again and said "well I am going to alter the letter head so there!"

"I shall not even try to stop you. If you derive pleasure from that, then so can I!"

CHAPTER 8

ANOTHER VISIT TO STELLAR TWO WITH A TWO DAY STOP OVER ON MARS

The visit to Stellar two was almost done on a single ship basis as costs were kept down. Judder however pointed out that the bulk of the cost was undercrew wages and these folk were going to be paid anyway albeit not at the premium rate they earned when actually in Space.

James Whistler had briefed Jarvis Kellar on his plans, and as an aside asked how he had got on with the dismissal of the two directors.

"They were unbelievably poisonous characters. When they read the letter they interpreted my promotion as a bribe and told me that I was a back stabbing rat! I know I am young enough to be hot headed but a backstabber, never   . I realised then looking back on my time on the board how skilfully you had dealt with them, and that I think was their undoing. They were so frustrated at not getting their own way, that they plied me with ideas that now looking back I see were flawed, and then when the chips were down and a show of hands was required, they hadn't even got the bottle to back me up! Looking back through their terms of engagement I see we would be within our rights to withhold diamond shard shipments to their company and I am minded to do just that. There surely must be other organisations that would dearly love to get their hands on a franchise for those!

"OK Jarvis, I think you are going along just nicely. If you invite the diamond shard franchise option, offer it wide including to the losers and we will see what becomes of that as they all compete for the rights to get in on the act. Make it known that any resignation from our board has to be permanent with no reinstatement. In other words any organisation wants to establish its credentials and good will the Space administration will vet all personnel carefully and that our decision on acceptance or removal is final!"

"Thank you James" he glanced up at the Whistler as he said his Christian name out loud and saw no untoward reaction and knew his life was about to undergo a sea change.

The Whistler then said "she is unattached you know!"

Jarvis Kellar was shocked at just how perceptive James Whistler was and said "I suppose its no use me asking who you mean then!" and smiled his appreciation. He had a date that night already arranged with Nancy Wisdom, and he thought that he would have to tell her that their little secret as he had thought of it simply wasn't a secret anymore. He smiled some more. He was going to be busy!

James   Whistler asked Helen to look after the technical details of the mission and decided that he would after all use a two ship mission. He looked into the duty rosters of the top six or seven Space captains and realised that Eric Whistler was due some leave. This suited his plan precisely because he felt he needed a top line man in reserve on the just in case basis and it had to be him Svensson or Johnson.

He planned to ask for volunteer crews and expected to be oversubscribed for a two ship mission. He asked for an excess stock of all the things required for mars and Stellar two, and four weeks later when the Gravitas and the Solar Orbiter were ready he had already put plans in place to second the Freeloader and the Moneybag if required so his mission was well backed.

He attended the pre-flight briefing and Captain Johnson asked if he would mind which ship he flew on. The Whistler had equal confidence in Captain Johnson and Henrik Svensson and so he didn't mind so he merely asked to go on the one carrying Judder.

Judder who had recently acquired his Captain's licence and now held the rank of Commander was set to fly as second in command to Henrik Svensson and so the die was set.

James Whistler felt heart stretching love pangs as he had to leave his beloved Josie behind, and she wept openly and begged to be allowed to re-join the undercrew. But he said no on the grounds that someone had a wedding to organise and such things were rarely done well by a man. She had no answer to that but knew she had been deftly controlled.

She was one tough bird as they say and soon accepted the state of affairs. Though after he had gone she suddenly thought of the time lapse anomalies and wondered what on earth she could confidently do about a date. Her answer was typical. She would arrange for a wedding at a registry office and keep changing the date if required until he got back. There would be time enough for a big splash later. She was content.

The early part of the journey went well and after a few days they were orbiting Mars. Mars had requested some items and these were docked from the ship's inventory as they were loaded onto shuttles.

The top four men spent some hours down on mars and were pleased to see that Ken Lee had done what he said and invested in farms. The expansion of mars population had slowed right down because there was no longer much immigration from earth. Some metalled roads were nearing completion and street lighting was now being installed. The atomic power station was fully functional and the logging of timber had just begun. Most of the trees were pines but something in the Martian soil; gave the wood considerable more hardness than earth pines and so they used this invaluable resource sparsely but increasingly.

Ken Lee had dedicated an Eden shelter, to climate adjustment and the following morning the four Space men went in there to breathe the thin air, after a half hour the outer door was opened and they walked outside to sample the Martian atmosphere. They were all very short of breath and though the oxygen level had risen to a decent percentage, the lower atmospheric pressure due to the smaller size of mars made hard physical graft almost impossible, at least it did to the Space crews. Ken admitted that he had used them as an experiment, because it was obvious that any number of Martian folk could manage better than the earth crew. "We are slowly adapting" Ken theorised.

"I think you are right" gasped Judder as he tried to walk along at a normal pace. Even with the reduced weight Judder found it difficult to walk any distance without pausing. Although a man weighed less on mars, the lower atmospheric pressure still made it hard work to adapt and the adaption period was now calculated to be several months.

After taking quick stock of the expansion on mars they took their leave to get on with the rest of their mission, the consensus of opinion on mars was that mars really was pretty well rowing its own boat and was basically a donator to, not a recipient from earth.

One could ask no more of a colony. (Not unless you were a blind in one eye politician), but hopefully the powers that be back on earth were finally seeing what and what was not reasonable.

The mission went to the first jump portal and both ships emerged unmarked near Pluto's orbit. Pluto itself was millions of miles away following its peculiar tilted orbit. The next jump was made and both ships exited without problem and in the distance was the binary sun of Stellar two. They checked on stellar two and found where she was in her orbit then used the gravity motors to get into geo stationary orbit above the planet. They listened to the mobile phone transmissions and heard nothing but static. There was no sign of life detectable and this worrying scene was the background to a four way head to head aboard the Gravitas.

Henrik Svensson commented "there is a large amount of cloud or opaque gas in the atmosphere; I saw no sign of that the last time we were here, and it may be so thick as to prevent mobile phone transmissions. The cloud covers the entire area where the settlers were and so things may be ok, but I don't like it!"

Captain Johnson asked if Heinrich was on this mission. He was and five minutes later he walked onto the bridge. "Good day gentlemen and just what are you after today!" he grinned.

"Herr Schmidt, Heinrich you are easily the most experienced away team leader that we have, what do you make of this?"

Heinrich looked at their records and said "I think we discovered a dormant volcano last time we did a survey, I wonder if it has erupted. That could account for the thick smoke in the atmosphere."

Judder frowned and said "I think we should send a six shuttle mission down there with us all suited up and bring all of the settlers back here if any are still alive!"

James Whistler smiled "let us not panic just yet. This bunch of folk is as resourceful as you will find, and may well have found some way to survive the problem that we are seeing. A six shuttle mission? Well

I agree with that. Ferrying them all back up here, well possibly, but we do need to go down and see what gives first!"

Captain Johnson gave his orders. "Six shuttles, Heinrich see to that and arm your men just in case. We will be able to take the entire population off the planet if we have to, we have spare capacity with the undercrews." He sniffed once then said "ok hop to it! Ah I just thought heat may be a problem if the atmospheric pollution is severe. Take some gas bottles and barbecue stoves if we have any."

The mission was soon under weigh with each shuttle only carrying two men to maximise the passenger carrying capacity. Fortunately due to the thoroughness of the previous mission the exact co-ordinates of the settlement were known. The shuttle pilots used this to position the shuttles above the camp and then they were all landed manually.

It was dark even though technically it was day time, and it was cold. There was a frost on anything at all with a sharp edge on it. The rescue mission soon found the village and the water in the upturned Eden shelter was frozen solid. Other Eden shelters were empty. Heinrich again led this foray and he muttered that the Captain had been correct in his notion that it would be cold. There was however no wind. Heinrich took a gas stove heater into one of the Eden shelters and lit it. The flames were longer and slower burning than in earth type atmospheres. It soon warmed the place up though, and he instructed his men to do the same in each of the other shelters close by. Now, one Eden shelter had been modified by the settlers who had effectively made three into one by a rather ingenious means. They had turned some of the adjoining fixing clamps round so that a horseshoe shaped enclosure was the result. Heinrich's team took three gas ring heaters into it and lit up. There was no sign of the settlers. All this information was relayed back to the main mission ships. Heinrich wondered whether the idea with the horseshoe shelter was an interrupted plan to make a ring, in effect a giant igloo.

They were still wondering why there were no signs of foot prints when suddenly a disturbance on the floor interrupted their thoughts. A large trap door was thrown back and the lithe figure of a settler sprang out. He turned grinned and said "you took your time!" within minutes he had explained how they had had these cold snaps before and had begun excavations under the Eden shelters and then decided to excavate first, and make a large cavern and top it with a ring of Eden shelters joined by a polythene sheet across the shelter tops. "We are all in this and one other ring shelter, but we finished that one, and we were just awaiting the atmosphere to clear and let a bit of light in then start up our lives again!"

He had a heavy beard and Heinrich exploded "Jack?"

He was relieved when Jack Robinson grinned and said "well if it ain't me old mucker Heinrich!"

The two men shook hands and Heinrich immediately offered a weeks respite aboard the space ships, but to his surprise the emerging settlers all declined to a man. They left the heaters going and with Jack set out to open up the other Eden ring.

This one had less folk and more livestock, and every one was in surprisingly fine fettle.

Heinrich then asked Jack how the hell, as he put it, had he got the runner beans back to earth.

Jack grinned "well I was just about to get my pilots licence for Space travel when I decided to throw my lot in with this bunch of saddos. I took a bag of our most recent bean progeny and took the shuttle off. I knew the co-ordinates for the jumps and I took the shuttle out to Uranus. I met with the Captain down on the diamond mine area and asked if he would get the beans to the Prof. None of us knew where he lived so I put on what I could and simply hoped for the best!"

"Well I have met the Prof but I have never been privileged enough to go to one of his parties, though I heard your beans got there and he will be planting them in a couple of months!"

Heinrich got on his communications transmitter. "Rescue mission leader here come in the Gravitas!"

"This is the Gravitas go ahead please!"

"The settlers are all alive and well and refuse to be rescued. Did I catch someone saying that you have something for them in the way of information?"

"If you mean letters from home we sure have!"

Jack Robinson's eyes lit up.

"I would come back up there with you right now if I can bring some letters back." Heinrich selected one of his pilots and asked "Fred would you like to ferry Jack up there and then bring him back with the mail?"

Jack was given a spare Space suit and within two hours had showered and shaved and presented himself to the bridge on board the Gravitas. A smiling Henrik Svensson gave him a drop of 'Space lubricant' and he asked Jack what was going on down on the planet. "We get these periodic thick cloud cover and when it happens it brings us winter for a couple of weeks. This time though it has been nearly five weeks and we are still in darkness. As a matter of fact after I used the shuttle to send the Prof some beans when I came back home I flew over the dormant volcano. Well it isn't dormant. And it blew some rock pieces up at me and caused damage to a fuel tank. I jettisoned the tank for safety and guess where it went—straight down the mouth of the volcano. I had by then flown past it and I landed without incident but hours later the smoke got up our noses and its been there ever since. Just before the rock flew up and damaged my tank I noticed that the walls of the volcano are very tall and thin and I have been wrestling with the idea of dropping another tank in there to try and collapse the rim in on itself!"

"Ok" said Henrik, "After you've gone back with this mail sack" he grabbed the bag from behind the seat, and shoved into Jack's hands, I shall go over to the Solar Orbiter and see what we can organise. Get your self back down there and our lads will stay with you any way. We have a huge amount of ordnance for you so it would be good if we can find some way to slow that volcano down. He's ready Fred!" he called out.

Two hours later the settlers were hungrily reading letters from friends and relatives. There were quite a few children on Stellar two and they were mystified as to why their parents were so engrossed in reading. Jack thought that this was good because the kids had no ties back to earth and did not miss it at all. Much less stress on the parents.

CHAPTER 9

VOLCANO PLUGGING

On the Solar Orbiter, Captain Johnson asked for James Whistler and Judder and Henrik to join him. The ships both orbited the planet but in different orbits to get a better picture of the erupting hole in the ground. It was not erupting as violently as earth volcanoes did but it produced a huge amount of particle debris. From time to time the smoke would waft away and they confirmed Jack Robinson's claim of very tall thin walls. They had a few explosives experts on board but they had never had bigger explosions than those required to bring down unsafe or unwanted buildings. James Whistler questioned each of these men until he thought he had squeezed all their technical knowledge from them then he made his conclusion.

He put the following proposal to the meeting.

"Gentlemen, I am a scientist, not an engineer. This would be a daunting task for any engineer but what I would like to do is to drop three charges down the throat of that volcano, simultaneously dropping five smaller charges round the outside of it the timing would be that the inner powder would blow first and the outer powder blow second but only a short time later. Now this would burn up all of the inflammable gases etc inside the ring and then when the shock wave of that had gone upwards possibly bending then cracking the walls the outer charges would push the walls from the outside. As the atmosphere responds to the charges shockwave it would blow the walls in on themselves and put a top on the eruption it would still allow the escape of gas but it would slow it down!"

Captain Johnson enquired as to the likelihood of success, but the Whistler did a Gallic shrug and said "even a good engineer would be struggling with that one and I am no engineer. I can only give it my best shot so to speak, I would suggest that we have a total and immediate evacuation procedure in place for our stellar two colonists in case it all goes horribly wrong!"

"Chances of success James?"

The Whistler blew out a long breath from between compressed lips and shook his head, "I am unable to give you even a remote guess, but I think it may be the only chance the settlers have. If that thing keeps on blowing debris out at its present rate it will put the entire planet into an ice age, and all our efforts up to the present will have been for nothing."

"Request whatever ordnances you require and get on with it. Good luck you are our only chance. Henrik and Judder- organise a fleet of shuttles and on big bang day, have every one sitting in them but take off only if we tell you to. Ok action stations!"

The Whistler went to the ships library room and found what he could on the use of explosives. Engineering is often seen as the illegitimate offshoot of science though it shared the elegant reasoning of the sciences. Any engineer considered his profession to be in a discipline that was the poetry of science. After a few hours the Whistler realised he had no chance of acquiring sufficient engineering knowledge overnight so he used history. He pondered the Dam Busters raid in the earlier half of the twentieth century, and he took on board the truth that Barnes Wallis had found and that was that the explosives were far more effective when close up to their target. The Whistler decided to drop two ten ton loads down the throat of the volcano and fifteen smaller one ton charges around the perimeter these would be dropped from above the volcano from geo stationary orbit. Each charge would initially be sent downwards by a small gunpowder rocket and the explosions would be triggered by long cat's whisker probes that would surround the smaller charges.

He slept on it.

He asked Judder to get together as many of the ships engineers as he could and then explained what he wanted to do. One of the engineers said, "You will need an altitude go-no-go zone so if the cat's whisker gets struck by a flying particle while it is still a couple of thousand feet up it will not trigger a premature explosion!"

James Whistler nodded "that job is yours then!" another voice piped up. "The outer charges need to be controlled in a clockwise or anti clock wise ring so that the tall walls don't collide with each other and jam when only half way down" "you got that bit then" said James.

A third voice then said I think the charges down the throat are a serious error. This volcano is not an earthly one and there does not seem to be a vast amount of explosive gas so I don't think there is anything to be gained by trying to clean the bowl out, in fact it may crack an already feeble bottom crust and cause a disastrous big eruption. I think you should drop only a single big bomb on the side where the walls are thinnest and the starting point for your circular blast should be near there, the idea being to get the big shock wave to arrive just after the weakening wall cracking shocks and thus improve your chances of blowing the wall down. Once part of it is gone the rest will fall more easily!"

James Whistler smiled hugely as if a huge weight had been lifted from his shoulders as in deed it had. "Well team lets get to it, Judder you know most of these guys and this time I assure you there will be no expert rushing in to take the credit, so you may have as many men as you like. I will square everything with Captain Johnson."

The Whistler knew that Judder was archly practical and he could tell from those who spoke up that they would do a better job than he could himself and he would have been pleased to give any help that he could, which in this case was almost nothing.

Five days later they had the explosives and their trigger devices set up. There was no room for a dress rehearsal they would either get it about right or not but the Whistler felt the sooner they did something the better.

Captain Johnson had quietly watched Judder's team and how each man conducted himself making mental notes of behaviour. Perhaps the cleverest of the bomb squad as he thought of them was at his best when he was arguing with those of a more practical nature. He understood more of the theory than his colleagues, but lacked their practical turn of mind. Judder soon quelled the little squabbles that broke out just as the Prof used to.

Captain Johnson stood and observed in wonder at this peculiar skill.

In the end there was the equivalent of one ten ton bomb and eight one tonners. The necessary shuttle evacuation procedure was enacted and much to the concern of the settlers they all had to concede and board the shuttles.

Up on the two ships the Solar Orbiter had made the ten ton bomb and this was huge, the other one tonners had been made aboard the Gravitas; the shuttles took the bombs down to about fifteen thousand feet and then let them go at their calculated times. The shuttles then sped away from the danger zone. The wall bombs unfortunately started their clockwise explosions and were just over half way round the volcano when the ten tonner went off. There was a huge blast and the other one tonners went off as they completed their tasks. The dust cleared from view but the volcano still stood exactly as before, up on the Solar Orbiter James Whistler stood glumly by, observing. Judder was in one of the shuttles with a pair of binoculars. He stared and stared but the walls remained intact. A sudden rumble could clearly be heard and an internal explosion had taken place, thus proving the technician's fear of a big eruption was well founded. A large chunk of rock shot outward but did not clear the volcano walls, after it collided with the inside of the walls, a crack appeared and then the first sign of movement as a section of the wall fell outwards, crashing down with massive force. The reaction to that was that another section of the wall fell inwards followed by another then another until the volcano had totally fallen in on itself except one peak which had defied all efforts and remained standing. The dust was clearing now and though there was still a rising plume it was only a minor amount.

Judder felt exultant but kept a calm voice as he said "shuttle nine reporting; tell the evacuation team to stand down." He and his pilot heard the cheers that rang through the mother ship.

Again the good luck that had generally followed efforts by the spacemen had been evident. The progression of the rock bashing, had really not gone according to plan, but the aim had been achieved.

Within two days the atmosphere had cleared and warmth began to return to the planets surface, leaving the colonists to go about their daily chores. Jack Robinson was the only one of the pioneers who knew just how lucky the volcano snuffing had been.

The final acts on this mission were about to unfold. The earth crews asked the settlers if they thought the eco-system could support any more livestock. The settlers asked if pigs could be provided and a number of these were donated by the Solar Orbiter. Time would tell if this would be a success.

Every move made on this mission had been thoroughly catalogued so that the Whistler would have as much data as possible to study as they tried to explain any time shifts that occurred.

The mission had withdrawn a vast amount of supplies from its stores for the colony and the shuttles delivered these to a compound set up for the purposes. The Solar Orbiter and the Gravitas stayed in orbit until a decent prediction of the planet's temperatures could be made. Conditions were returning to normal. A few more fish were released into the oceans. The colonists were certain that they had seen a shoal of some size and expected to be able to harvest some in the near future. Both magpies and squirrels had survived the cold weather, and two chickens had also escaped. These too had survived, so the settlers had high hopes for the pigs.

The trees planted by the settlers survived the mini- winter they were just coming out of and some mosses had begun to appear on the damp spots on numerous rocks. As an experiment, snails, beetles and spiders were introduced along with a species of fly. The settlers allocated the management of this project to one of their botanists. The botanist introduced all of these species to pools at the ocean's edge. He had noted that the planets water was only mildly salty, and thought that he could accelerate evolution, by providing a suitable environment. He knew he might be wrong but promised to keep a careful log of events ready for analysis on the next visit to the planet.

Heinrich organised another two spatially stationary satellites for telecommunications purposes so that the planet would have virtually complete cover, except for the Polar regions. The signals would be weak but as there was no other competing signals it was hoped that the settlers could explore the whole planet over the next few years.

The next few weeks were spent offloading the ordnances from the two ships. The time for the departure was fast approaching. Stellar 2 suddenly acquired another young life and Captain Johnson went to see the lady in question who was still in her confinement.

He left a small penknife as a birthday gift for the newcomer, who was a boy.

"I shall call him Kingdom!" declared the mother.

Kingdom Johnson relaxed as he realised that the name did indeed have a ring about it, and he was suddenly struck with wonder as to why he had hidden his name for so long.

Just before the return mission got under weigh, James Whistler asked if they could call at Triton and collect some new diamond shards for analysis.

CHAPTER 10

HOMEWARD BOUND

The Captain used the computor to decide his vectors and entered these into the ships navigation system so that after the first jump to the Pluto area he would make an additional mini-jump to the Triton area.

A visit was made to the diamond shard collection area on Triton, and James Whistler collected some samples. The miners had made their encampment around the outside edge of the hotspot and this provided the miners with sufficient heat for comfortable existence. The miners had a fortnightly visit from the Moneybag, and could easily collect the required tonnage of shards in that time and thus they lead a relaxed working schedule. Almost miraculously as shards were collected they were replaced by new ones growing as if by magic, and so the source of these was not going to disappear after just a few years. The Moneybag also brought the ordnances that the miners required and acted as a ferry for holiday entitled miners.

The rest of the homeward journey was boringly routine.

Back on earth in his laboratory James Whistler pondered the vast amount of data that had been collected, but first he checked on the passage of time on earth and the passage of time on his mission. In this instance they were almost identical. *Almost.*

When he compared his newly acquired data to data retrieved from previous missions he found that there had been a massive difference between registered time on earth compared to the mission time.

Purely because his latest mission, with meticulously recorded data had recorded a minor time shift he was driven to conclude that there really was a force out there in Space that grafted a time shift onto the missions. He noticed that the latest mission had recorded more time away than earth had, whereas all of the other missions using the jump had a time difference the other way. That was to say the earth time recorded was longer than the mission time recorded. He searched for means whereby his clocks on board the ship could make an erroneous reading and concluded that they did not have one. He knew that Helen's theory of inverse time had been shown to prove that a very long earth time could pass if you tried to exit the rethe too soon. No one had yet tried to stay in the rethe for say a year before attempting an exit. Helen's theory predicted a very short amount of time would have passed on earth, but this did need to be proven. It didn't need a year but perhaps a month was essential. All of this conjecture still left him with an essential nub. The nub was that you could do what you like in Space travel and earth time would proceed. The amount of earth time that passed would depend on what you did while you were in the rethe, but it would always go forward. You could manoeuvre yourself so that a greater or lesser time would pass, but this was strictly not time travel at all. You couldn't recover expended time.

What might reveal some element of time travel was the bars of metal experiment.

Obviously there were primeval forces at work trying to force the metals from one Space time continuum to another so more such experiments were needed.

The Whistler decided he would share his notions with Helen Svensson. Helen listened and agreed with the Whistler. It was looking decreasingly likely that real time travel would be possible. Helen suggested another party at the Prof's but James Whistler reminded her he had a wedding in only four days time and he would have to see to all that first.

Helen had got to know Josie Langan quite well during the time the mission to Stellar 2 was ongoing. Josie always started the day with a ritual, beginning in Helen's office then on through the Whistler's office and so through her round. As the cleaning lady she heard vast amounts of rumour. The latest being about Jarvis Kellar. If Josie knew then Helen would shortly know. Her latest, piece of information was that Nancy

Wisdom and Jarvis Kellar were an item, so she was a little surprised that Helen already knew.

"How on earth did you know that before I did?" she grinned.

"Your intended practically shoved them together. I think he likes the idea of the stability we women can bring, and having so recently turned your world upside down, he really did move things along particularly after he translated the little contre-temps in the canteen just before the last mission. By the way how are the wedding plans going?"

Josie Langan's face fell. "Haven't you had your invite yet?" she wailed, "Christ I might have forgotten to post it!"

"Don't panic, of course we have and I've replied so when is it?"

"The end of next week!"

Suffice it to say that the day came and went without incident. Josie invited one or two guests that none of the Space team knew but she also invited Heinrich. Heinrich had not quite been her boyfriend but had helped her enormously when she first joined the Space service undercrew.

The Prof was best man and he stood to make the customary speech beginning with the opening line---- "ladies and gentlemen I have heard praise in deed today. I have heard several of you complementing the chef saying that the meal is almost as good as those that I cook. Well for what it is worth I agree so please raise your glasses to Nancy Wisdom. Oh and by the way I think you can all guess where the runner beans came from" he paused while the chuckles died down. "These beans were indeed the produce of my garden. The seeds were sent to Stellar 2 and the progeny from there was returned to me. That is why the beans themselves are such a marvellous colour. Don't worry we have been eating them for weeks so none of you are guinea pigs!"

The Prof was a marvellous speech maker and ten minutes later he toasted the bride and groom.

James Whistler stood for the usual groom's speech but he motioned Josie to stand beside him, and then encircled her waist with his long arm. He only spoke a few words but there was not a dry eye in the place as he resumed his seat. Josie remained standing.

"James has had a hole in his life formerly filled by his first wife. I count myself unlucky never to have known her. I will try to fill that void in my own way, and I dare say that from time to time I will have to remind him not to devote so much time to his mistress- the Space Administration. Slightly alarmed expressions relaxed into affirmative nodding.

"I tried every which way to get to know him, all to no avail. He never even noticed me, and yet when I did finally ask him what he thought he was looking at, as I saw him eying me up, I had agreed to our first date in barely a few seconds. Ladies and gentlemen I give you my husband--- a mighty fast worker!"

James Whistler for once did not squirm as the spontaneous applause rang out; he just sat with a wide grin on his face.

Later on as some guests drifted off home the Prof asked the Whistler how the latest Space studies were progressing.

The Whistler told him that Helen was up to date on that but he for once was going on honeymoon and the world could go hang itself for a fortnight. The Prof smiled as he remembered his own honeymoon that was spent part at home and part in Gloucestershire helping Liz to sell up. The Whistler was off to sunnier climes and planned to do some walking and swimming and fishing. Mrs Whistler aka Josie Langan chimed in "yeah well I think he will walk to the poolside bar, then swim off to a table and then order some fish from the restaurant!"

The Whistler's closing remarks before heading to the honeymoon suite was to Jarvis Kellar. "Jarvis, watch out for those slimy characters because while I am away they will make a move if they have planned one!"

"Ok James, I have cultivated a few contacts while you have been away so let them try. I do try to not underestimate them but I think they may have underestimated me!"

With that the newly weds went off up to their room.

CHAPTER 11

SOME DEVELOPMENTS

Note from Catherine Whistler. As you may recall Jane Johnson has been helping me with the Space library work for some time now. We are not the scientists of the outfit but we discuss some of the interesting elements between us and apply our reasonable intellects to the issues.

One day at one of our frequent meetings Jane suddenly piped up, "When you sat in on that meeting a little while back and gave them all a printout taken from your secretarial notes, did you know that the printer in the kitchen also spewed the report out?"

"No I didn't at the time but from these records I do now, it hasn't caused a security issue has it?"

"No, no nothing like that but it set me thinking and because of that I haven't stopped thinking! I made a positive contribution to the amalgamated bars mission and since then I have engaged with you on all of the issues involved."

I must admit that I really enjoyed Jane's conversation and particularly enjoyed expressing my views to her.

She continued, "the reason I mention this now is because when we talk you have a good enough grasp of the goings on to add to my own understanding and I have also followed some of the lines of thought emanating from our little chats!"

"Well go on then!" I said.

"As you know, the Prof and Judder don't get bogged down with grand overall scientific principles or become distracted by the ferocious studying required on some microscopic detail. The freedom from those strictures allows them to function and make a contribution. Often the Whistler and Helen tidy up the notions and construct full blown theories from the basic notions postulated. This is team work at its best."

I grinned and invited her to come to the point before I died of curiosity.

She grinned in return and continued "I think we have need of another element in the study of time travel. You and I could be the Judders of the female world, I am not a mathematician but I can remember from my studies that if you need to explain something, you introduce a factor into an equation that is only there to explain what you want to prove. You then do all the maths involved and see if the idea is self supporting or not. If the original supposition is wrong then your theory falls about your ears. If it is correct then it can be developed further. Basically all this waffle is put to you Catherine to see if you agree that we should introduce an element that goes clockwise or anticlockwise according to whether time is added to our clock or subtracted from our clock. Then all we have to do is find out what influences this factor and we will be able to calculate how and where time elements get modified. Now just for good measure I think that all of our conjecture is based upon reasoning done in the ether. In my view the rethe as conceived by Helen is only a border between a world of negative time and a world of positive time, and it thus has zero time itself; we live in the positive time world. The reasons that I think this are Sonny and FB1. There is a reaction going on and James Whistler has already postulated that the outer layers of Sonny for example merely acts as a store for the heat provided and possibly some minor contribution to the reaction, and that he presumed that there was an equal and opposite reaction 'on the other side'.

I think he had only half grasped the nub there. I think that the rethe is an almost clear dividing line between the clockwise and anticlockwise existences and that here and there, there are bubbles of half and half which explains Sonny and FB1!"

"Jane, I should get all of that written down and I think that we two should demand another party at the Prof's place! It would be a turn up for the books if we could have answers cut and dried before James gets back from honeymoon!"

Jane smirked deliciously and then as a complete aside suddenly asked me if I had noticed anything about her husband recently. I thought about it and casually remarked that many more people were using his real name now.

She smacked her own forehead with the heel of her hand and said "Yes that's it, I knew there was something. Sometimes when I am trying to attract his attention he only responds to 'Kingdom' he has almost stopped responding to 'Cap'. I'm sorry about the sudden change of subject but I have been meaning to ask you that for a while but I always forgot!"

I picked up the phone and dialled Helen's number a few seconds later and she was on.

"Hi, Cathy what can I do for you?"

"hello Helen, you can organise another party at the Prof's place and if you want to know why you can get yourself across to Jane's place sometime in the coming week and all will be explained!"

I could feel her smiling as she said "Right, leave that with me!" we chatted about this and that but I was careful to reveal nothing, and finally turned to look at Jane as I put the phone down.

Jane had a look I had never seen before and I realised that I had put her firmly in the spotlight and she was nervous about it.

"Oh dear, sorry Jane but your idea was so exciting I got carried away for a moment!"

Jane raised philosophical eye brows and said "well the wheels are in motion now so that is that!"

Nine days later Liz welcomed them all into her home.

CHAPTER 12

JANE'S IDEAS ARE FLOATED

Helen had been round to Jane's and so knew what was afoot and was inwardly excited about the notion.

The girls involved all noticed the subtle as well as the obvious changes to the Prof's abode as he settled into the evening of his life with Liz. The usual pleasantries were exchanged but there was haste to get down to the business in hand.

This time the strains of "what a swell party this is" were absent as all the ladies knew that it was them that held centre stage, and a strange nervousness pervaded the atmosphere.

Helen had advised Jane to produce individual copies of her thesis for all concerned and every person there and there were some new partygoers, amongst whom was none other than Heinrich Schmidt.

Heinrich had of course been Jane's immediate superior when she was last an active crewmember. Jane smiled and gave him an affectionate kiss and welcomed him to the party.

"I shall be the envy of the whole Space service if I manage to get some of the Prof's magic beans down me!" he grinned. English had become the natural Space language and Heinrich had spoken it for so long now that his accent had almost gone.

Every party goer was sat round the large table in the Prof's living room, and the Prof stood up and asked for silence. You could hear a pin drop. "The floor is yours Jane" he said and sat down.

Jane's legs wobbled as she stood and against her expectation she saw the funny side of her predicament, and suddenly chuckled. "Ok that's the nerves out of the way!" she said.

"Ladies and gentlemen, I know most of you have read the little dissertation in front of you, and we will go through that on a point by point basis.

I expressed my views on how the last metal alloying mission should proceed and I was encouraged that my idea was taken up, and that little idea seems to have spawned many others. I have been helping Catherine Whistler to archive the Space reports in the Space library, and until I did that I had no idea just what a complex system was required to keep tabs on all of the goings on. Catherine was and is my best friend and confidant and she told me that we should demand another party at the Prof's place. Well she did just that and propelled me into my present position. Thank you very much Catherine!" there was a muted ripple of laughter from the assembly.

"Cathy and I discussed the reports between us and don't forget that we have to archive every report and opinion on anything reported and so we probably get a better overall picture than any one else.

Based on snippets from here and there an idea began to form in my mind, and the longer it stayed the tougher it became to ignore until finally I expounded my thesis to Catherine. It will almost certainly take mathematicians such as Helen and James to tidy the idea up, but I hope to appear to be the female Judder amongst us!"

As Jane drew breath Helen spoke up. "I have had time to consider this notion and I find it quite exciting. I had considered the ether to be an outer ball with a path through to an inner ball that I called the rethe, but Jane's idea implies that there is no inner or outer ball and yet still there are connections from one to the other. Jane's idea that the rethe is a fairly narrow divide between the two leaving the odd ragged bit causing the existence of things like Sonny is I am sure correct. Everything that we know is finite but we are into the realms of infinity or at least virtual infinity, and I think we may need a new branch of mathematics to deal with the concepts. I am a polished mathematician but I tell you in all honesty and candour that I wish the Whistler was here right now!"

Jane resumed her lecture. "From all of the data received so far it is abundantly clear that though in our clockwise existence we can expect to compress or stretch time it is still always going forward. I have formed the idea that in the anticlockwise world time will also be a malleable commodity but will always be going backwards compared to our concepts. The rethe is a neutral zone where the two concepts of time meet and exactly cancel each other out, apart from the fact that the interface generates the inverse time function as perceived by Helen. From observed behaviour we note that when we enter the rethe, we leave a trail tale behind so when we exit it our heading is unchanged. We also note that the journeys through the rethe are dead straight and not part orbital. We don't actually travel faster than light but we side step normal laws of physics for a short while and then reattach ourselves to them as we exit the rethe. Helen somehow deduced that there is an inverse function with regard to time when we do that. Should we ever find how to penetrate the rethe and emerge into the anticlockwise side then perhaps the numerator or denominator of our equations will have changed sign, or will have become an imaginary quantity, as is used extensively in modern day engineering.

The reason I lay claim to being a female Judder is that Judder here and his father before him have come up with notions that have enabled people like James and Helen to proceed along avenues of thought not otherwise obvious even to top scientists.

I offer my little thesis to the meeting to be attacked trodden on and so forth and I really hope that a new avenue is open for us all!"

As she sat down Captain Johnson lead the applause and then stood." Now you can all see why I married her!" the applause continued for a few seconds more but the Prof stood and intervened. "Guests I think now is a good time for our first tea break, let the ideas sink in and see if you can think of some stinking questions!"

They broke up for coffee and sandwiches. Jane sought out Heinrich and asked him how he was.

"Hello Jane, I am absolutely fine. I always wanted to come to one of these dos because in the Space service it always improves your street cred! I got quite friendly with Josie Langan a few years ago when she needed some help and I managed to curb my baser instincts while she recovered from her marriage disaster. It was good job she recovered because she is an attractive woman and I couldn't hold out indefinitely!"

"Yes she mentioned some time ago that you had been a great help to her and I am sure she would have asked you to one of these parties herself before too long. Who asked you this time?"

"It was Catherine Whistler, and she presumed it might be nice for you to have your erstwhile commanding officer at your side!"

"Catherine again. I tell you there are a number of people here today that owe her a big vote of thanks!" she looked at Heinrich but his mouth was almost agape.

"Who is that heavenly creature over there?" he nodded towards a young girl.

The magic seems to be working again thought Jane as she beckoned Queenie over and made the introductions. "Heinrich Schmidt commander of the first mission to see extra-terrestrial life, may I introduce you to Queenie, the first human being conceived and born away from earth!"

Queenie was just eighteen and blushed to the roots of her hair. Heinrich, who was just in his thirties, casually took her elbow and taking a glass of orange juice smoothly from a tray ushered Queenie off to a quieter corner.

The party never returned to the formal lecture style but individual guests asked Jane questions directly.

Reverend William Jackson asked her where god fitted into all this. Jane thought for a moment and said "well perhaps god has his head in our side and the devil has his in the other side. Or perhaps god and the devil are head and tail of the same entity. Perhaps god and the devil exist like Sonny and oscillate rapidly from one side to the other, and maybe that is why god gave us free will so that we can side with whichever we choose!"

William Jackson smiled and withdrew to consider what she had said. He was intrigued by some of the notions and wondered what some religious zealots would make of these new ideas. His wife Hannah was talking to Catherine Whistler when Jane wandered over and joined in the conversation. During a lull she told Hannah that she had been probed on the question of god and what she had offered as a possible explanation. Hannah Jackson beamed. "He is not a godly man but he is a spiritual man. He sees past the walls erected by zealots. He will ponder what you have said and he will be back to you on it, on that you can depend!"

Jane wandered over to the Prof and Liz.

"I see a few feminine touches here and there!" she said. Elizabeth smiled and said "Told you!" the Prof held his hands up in smiling surrender. "The changes are so subtle I didn't think anyone would notice!" he said.

Jane laughed and said "For all your legendary perception you can't hold a candle to a woman in the home!"

After about another hour of circulating she found herself talking to Brian and Nadine Judd. "Answered any awkward questions yet?" enquired Judder.

"Surprisingly few!" admitted Jane.

"That is because you have scored a bull's-eye, that's why. I can smell it. I can always smell it when somebody gets something right! You wait till James gets back he will tell you!"

"I haven't sent him a copy yet, I couldn't do that while he is on honeymoon!" smiled Jane.

"Ah!" said Judder looking guilty.

"Mister subtle strikes again!" grinned Nadine.

"Oh well if the cat is out of the bag, it is out of the bag. I suppose he would have been back anyway in a couple of days so it won't make him change his flights or anything! reasoned Jane.

"Erm Nancy got a minute?" she enquired as Nancy Wisdom was scooting past. Nancy stopped and apologised for not speaking sooner only she had a worried look on her face. "It is that poisonous bunch that James got rid of, they are giving Jarvis a hard time, and he is on the phone as we speak!"

For some reason this really got under Jane's skin and she marched across to Jarvis and snatched his phone off him. "This is Jane Johnson here" she snarled. "Identify yourself immediately!" the erstwhile hawk director on the other end of the line was caught off guard as he new full well that Captain Johnson would not be far away and he was far too cowardly to risk upsetting him, "well I"—he began but Jane boiling with rage now cut him off "listen to me you little turd, there have been substantial developments while you have been away, you are out of the loop by your own actions, any information that you have is so far out of date as to be laughable. Call a board meeting at your company and invite me to attend to discuss all of your grievances and be prepared to face the casualties of war. Now get off the line and don't ever interrupt a party thrown by me again!" she gave Jarvis his phone back with trembling fingers, and then realised in a flash that it was the hall phone of her own house. She was numb with rage.

Jarvis Kellar beckoned Captain Johnson over and said, "I hope what your wife just said will do the trick because I have just discovered that the two men thrown off the board have underground connections to the mob, and they have applied immense pressure onto me with death threats and the like during the last two days, and I dearly hope that nothing untoward will happen as a result!"

Captain Johnson beckoned the Prof and outlined the recent event.

"Who would be the best man to get onto this do you think?"

Without a moments hesitation the Prof said "Fordy!"

Captain Johnson realised that there had been a substantial hole in his logic when he played his part in arranging the world constitution structure. He had known that the Donkey had stripped the wealth of many of the rich but he had not thought of the mob. As he pondered things it became an obvious oversight that he had not considered how the Donkey had gained influence so quickly. It couldn't possibly be all down to electoral disenchantment, so there must have been organised wealth behind it. The mob- and it was flexing its muscles again.

It was time to move quickly but to do what?

The party began to break up but the Prof organised a meeting between himself, Fordy, Captain Johnson and Jarvis Kellar.

CHAPTER 13

FORDY COMES TO THE MEET

Fordy turned up with his twin brother Peter, and introductions were made.

"I thought you knew that it was mob money underwriting the Donkey!" he said.

"For once I was totally naïve!" admitted Captain Johnson.

Jarvis Kellar outlined the brief history of his elevation to his present position and what had happened whilst James Whistler was away. "The culmination of this is that I have now received serious death threats and I think that Captain and Mrs. Johnson are in mortal danger too!" Jarvis Kellar frowned.

Fordy had kept silent for a while. "I still have contacts with the darker side" he admitted "but I think this situation is far more serious than you realise. The governments are still weak but the mob has recovered its strength quickly, and it is greedy. May I suggest that you reinvent the resistance but don't use any of these men." He scribbled a few names down.

The Prof read the names and was surprised at some of those at the top of the list.

"Their little nests of agitators are compromised either by mob involvement or mob influence and so really must not be used!"

Captain Johnson suddenly admitted that it had been remiss of him not to keep in touch after the reformation because Fordy had played a major role in bringing the Donkey down.

Fordy smiled, "Neither me nor Peter here has any major whinges at the moment but we might have if the mob is allowed an unchecked rise again. Remember that the mob is family run and these guys are not like half baked politicians, there is a centuries old tradition and discipline running through their operations. The only weak link that I have been able to find is that their money now all comes through Swiss banks, and the transactions are done in bullion. The mob won't trust paper money."

The five men all pondered that, with five minds trying to imagine how they would wrest the money from the mob's hands and then where could they take it afterwards.

Captain Johnson's mind began exploring another path. "These men who are making life uncomfortable for us at the moment are not men of hard steel. In a way they really lack bottle so what is someone like that doing fronting the mob? Is it that they are just corrupt and have made promises that they cannot keep and now find themselves facing a very short future? I have seen men like this before and they would have retired to lick their wounds long ago, but seeing as they haven't done that, another malign influence has been brought to bear upon them.

No, I think our course is clear we must befriend these men, find out their links and then remove the links. Fordy do you have contacts with many of the resistance fighters still?"

"Who else do you think we drink with at night?" he grinned, "and by the way that cough never returned, so I really do owe you one there. That impromptu speech you made that turned me that night has remained with me and I am glad to say that you have achieved a good proportion of the half promises, but all that could be compromised by the mob. In fact the whole world order could be up for grabs again if the mob gets the upper hand!"

"It is different this time because we can always blame grontlewich can't we?" chuckled Captain Johnson.

The Ford twins permitted themselves a wry smile. Captain Johnson then gave Peter Ford a letter from those he left on Titan. Peter opened the letter and thanking Captain Johnson for it began to titter as he read.

He gave it to Fordy to read while he explained that there were a number of fallen bigwig politicians in jail there. The letter accused them all of being the slowest learners of anybody, but said that after life on the outside of the little jail community they all found life easier once they threw their lot wholly into the prison life.

"Whatever we do we must not send any mob members up there or they would ruin the place!" ejaculated the Prof.

"I would like to think you are wrong but I fear you could be right" said Peter Ford. Life up there changed my outlook completely but I think a real mobster would try to make it a mob colony.

Fordy stood up and said "I would like to meet these men who are causing trouble. I need to assess their characters before any other move is made, and of course with a bit of prodding they might just reveal who is pulling their strings!"

CHAPTER 14

JANE HAS TO PUT HER MONEY WHERE HER MOUTH IS

The Whistler and his new bride were due back tomorrow, but when Helen went through her usual chore of opening E-mail and post she found a savagely worded demand that Jane Johnson attend a meeting at this corporation's head quarters to explain her words.

Helen got an indignant reply off within seconds. 'Jane Johnson is not an employee of the Space administration in any way shape or form, and by what right did this corporation imagine they could send such a demand? Only a letter from your chairman will be deemed of sufficient weight to gain a reply!'

The reply to this when it came was of a completely different tenure. The chairman himself began by apologising for the crass and overbearing language used in the letter.

He understood why Jane Johnson had been so upset and in line with her forcefully worded request, invited her to attend a meeting so that the air could be cleared.

Helen immediately realised that this letter so much more polite than the original may be a sign of physical danger to Jane. Within minutes both Jane and Kingdom were aware of the position.

Jane was a rather deep person and was not easily upset but she bridled immediately. Captain Johnson assumed his full professional calm and moments later had Fordy on the mobile explaining the position.

Fordy's response was reassuring "well that gives me a chance to get to see the directors involved. I've already found out who the contact with the mob is and he is drunk out of his skull just now due to an accidental overdose of something or other" he said vaguely. "Go along with the demand and I will get to the director posing as another mob contact, I got the contact code from the drunk just before he became too drunk to remember it, - I hope!"

Some people like Frank Kowalski had that courage that only shows when it is a backs to the wall situation. Jane was placid in the extreme but once roused would face a lion with her bare hands and she was roused now.

There were more acidly worded e-mails going back and forth, but Jane drove to the corporation and almost bit the head of the security man off when he wanted her to wait while he cleared her security. He recognised her anger and raised the barrier warning his boss that there was a mad woman on the way in. Fordy was already there and had observed. He grinned in shear admiration at the way she physically dominated the gateman and then grabbed the erstwhile hawk director as he was on his way to the meeting.

"What the hell is going on?" he demanded. "I am your substitute contact and they only use me when an execution is about to take place. Your contact code is XJS 994W."

The director suddenly went deathly pale and confessed that though he had tried everything he knew, he had been unable to get re-elected to the Space administration honorary directors list. "I have tried every trick clean and dirty but I have got no where!" his words were sticking in his mouth as his mouth ran dry.

"You've got an exaggerated idea of your own importance, they don't send me to deal with the likes of you!" snarled Fordy. "There must be another higher ranking man in the firing line, who is it?"

He watched as the director tried to swallow and he offered a shot in the dark. "It is either your chief executive or chairman!" Fordy watched the eyes and as he said chairman there was a definite flicker. "Ok so it is the chairman" said Fordy.

"I never divulged that!"

"Not in so many words you didn't that is true! I will offer advice and throw you a lifeline. Get me into the building and I will let you go. You just run and don't ever come back. Take me into the area where the meeting takes place and then run!"

Moments later Fordy had been issued with a security pass and was taken up to the top floor and along to an office. The glass door was just swinging shut behind Jane as she walked into the lion's den. Fordy stuck his foot in the door and heard the cordial greeting spoken to Jane as the chairman welcomed her in.

"Ok, run!" he hissed and watched as the director made his exit down the fire escape.

Fordy walked calmly in and put a finger across his smiling lips to warn the secretary to be quiet. She saw his security badge and relaxed, smiling in return. He sidled over to her desk being careful not to come into the chairman's field of view.

"Solid looking, these glass doors" he said.

"Bullet proof" she replied.

"Bullet proof?" Fordy ejaculated, "What the hell goes on here?"

"Two white coffees please Imelda and no sugar!" squawked the intercom. Imelda walked across to the machine and made four coffees and set two down on her table. She pressed the door release button and took two coffees in. She was surprised by the angry and determined look on Jane Johnson's face, but withdrew politely as any experienced PA would. She resumed her seat and began chatting to Fordy. He was charmed by her and realised that she was gently pumping him. He smiled inwardly and was pleased to notice that her discarded earphones gave her audible contact with the chairman's office. He could barely hear but could hear enough to tell that the temperature of the conversation was slowly rising. The chairman had imagined that he would be able to simply charm Jane Johnson to his point of view knowing that she had contacts within the Space administration. It would all be so easy then to bring about a bit of back door influence, except that it wasn't. Jane angrily asked him how he would feel if life threatening remarks were received on his house phone. He knew in that instant that his bungling man had gone too far.

"Imelda, get Elliman up here instantly!"

"He hasn't registered in yet chairman" she intoned.

"I bet he's still running!" thought Fordy.

"Do you take me for a complete fool?" demanded Jane. "It is the easiest thing in the world to make a subject changing statement like that and I don't care whether you sack him six times or whatever else you do, no one is going to make death threats against a guest in my house. I had hoped to find some way out of this mess but you corporate types think you can do and say what you like to whomsoever. You can't!" she said, stood up spun on her heels and walked towards the glass doors. Fordy glanced across at the coffee machine and saw the chairman reflected in the chromium of the machine as he opened a draw and pulled something out. Fordy took no chances and he hit the door open button on Imelda's little console and leapt across and into the office and threw Jane Johnson to one side just as the chairman levelled what appeared to be a dart gun at her. Fordy fired his ready drawn weapon and registered the look of surprise on the chairman's face as the bullet entered his brain.

Imelda was shocked, and just sat there. Fordy helped an equally shocked Jane Johnson to her feet saying "Imelda I think you are a smasher, you deserve better than this. You have almost just witnessed a gangland killing. Give me ten minutes to get Mrs. Johnson to a safe place then ring the police and give them the following code number- XJS994W. He checked and satisfied himself that she had written it down properly.

Fordy retrieved the dart gun and then scarpered.

In his car he used his hands free and reported in to Captain Johnson, giving him the essence of what had been said.

One very unhappy Captain Johnson listened later on as Fordy gave him full details of the morning's escapade. He surmised that the chairman's failure to persuade Jane to his view would have resulted in her being drugged, taken by some pseudo ambulance and then used as a bargaining chip. Captain Johnson was distraught and privately wondered if he would have had the moral courage to withstand the pressure that this would undoubtedly have brought about. Suddenly he realised just why the mob had always been so successful, and with the diamond shards being so massively expensive the attraction to the mob was patently obvious.

"So what about the other resignee?" he voiced his worry.

Fordy acquainted him with the situation regarding Elliman. Later that morning a smiling James Whistler put in an appearance. The smiles died as soon as he heard of the latest shenanigans.

He was philosophical but realised that all senior members of the Space administration were at risk.

Jane Johnson fully recovered from her ordeal told the Whistler just how she had been outraged as she watched Jarvis Kellar doing his best to shield them all, then realised as she handed a phone back to Jarvis Kellar that the threats were an incoming call on her house phone.

"Well you sure precipitated a rapid response!" he smiled.

Fordy listened and then told them how he had played a part in getting the normal mob contact drunk and had managed to get his contact code number before he passed out. He also told them of how he had given this code number to Imelda and expected her to give it to the police if she was clean. Two days later a small section in a local paper related to finding a body riddled with bullets but with no identifying marks or paperwork, but just enough detail to reveal that Imelda had called the police. Fordy had a certain satisfaction knowing that Imelda at least was straight. He wondered though how many more tendrils the mob had reaching into the business world and suggested that an investigation into mob connections be made as a condition of employment within the Space administration.

Fordy suggested that a separate security organisation needed to be employed to protect the interests of all concerned. He could see that the mob wanted in, and if they ever got in they could wreak havoc with the Space service or even the world particularly if they got hold of nuclear weapons.

James Whistler made an offer. He asked Fordy if he and his brother would consider heading up such an organisation. Fordy smiled, then chuckled then roared with laughter.

James Whistler was dismayed "you might at least have considered it" he grumbled.

Fordy catching his breath said "well of course we would be delighted, but surely you can see the irony here. My brother almost became a Space floating pork chop, and I was second in command in the dreaded Donkey era. You've got to say that's a real turn around!"

The Whistler did see and he began to reluctantly grin in his turn. "every job we asked you to do whilst you were in the resistance, you made a go of it, and your brother against all expectations became chairman of the Titan jail colony, so you are both blessed with ability and courage, and I dare say if it was not generally known that there are two of you that fact could be turned to advantage from time to time."

Fordy, still chuckling added "I am virtually certain that I can speak for my brother but I must offer him the chance to decline so I will be in touch."

Just a few hours later the phone rang, "James Whistler!" he mumbled through a sandwich.

"Peter Ford here, we will be delighted to accept but we need a couple of days to in effect design our company. We will need to employ at least half a dozen men and so it won't be cheap, can we meet say in three days time?"

"Did you laugh as much as your brother when he put my idea to you?"

"Probably more, it really is something of a turn around, but it should just fill the need in my life to be doing something so on behalf of both of us I thank you. I fell into the pit of iniquity with the Mule, and Don did the same with the Donkey, and so neither of us wants the same thing from the mob. We have learnt a hard lesson there. I will be in touch. Bye."

James Whistler put the phone down, then picked it up and dialled the Prof.

"James Whistler here and before you ask I enjoyed every minute of my honeymoon!"

"Ok James. It looks as if we are all going to need improved security. It was me that recommended Fordy and I gather he has started how he means to go on!"

"Yes, Bill he made a fantastic start, and it was solely down to him that Jane escaped the clutches of the mob. I think the commercial value of anything from Space has been overlooked by the mob until now and so I think we are in for a tough time. I am ringing to ask what you think remuneration levels should be for our security. I have just asked the Ford brothers to set up a security organisation with them at its head, and I think I cannot afford to be mean about it otherwise the mob will simply tempt them with money!"

"It could be as much about status as money you know, what I would do is to ask them what they require in terms of money and simply double it. Give them some influence at your board level and a few shares in your organisation!"

"Yes I was thinking that they could or rather should have a seat on our board so that they could assess the risk involved with any strategy that we embark upon. Ok Prof, solid advice as usual. How is every one? I gather you had a party without me!"

"Go to the Johnson's and get Jane to expound her thesis to you and you will see what I mean. I take it you've read her dissertation?"

"Yes it looks good to me!"

"Both Judder and I are certain she has opened an avenue every bit as exciting as Helen's idea of the rethe if not more so, but Jane gives it something else when she speaks. It would be worth your while I assure you!"

"I think I will do that. Helen is handling the day to day things with her usual skill so I've got a couple of days until our security service starts up, I'll do it now! Bye."

Two minutes later he had made his arrangements and had told Josie.

That evening they rolled up at the Johnson's.

CHAPTER 15

THE WHISTLER LISTENS TO JANE

"Hello James, happy?" said Jane as she welcomed the newly weds in. "I would absolutely love a rattle with Josie but I gather you are going to give me an ear bashing instead, aren't you James?"

James Whistler smiled as he waited for Josie to follow him in. "The night is yet young and I do not think I will get away from here until you and Josie have had your girlie chat!"

They all sat down for a coffee and Kingdom Johnson said "well Josie Langan now Whistler, I think you and I are to be sidelined this evening, I heard that you can play a piano. If that is true perhaps you can knock a tune out of mine. Frankly I can't play a note!" with that he deftly escorted Josie into the other large downstairs room and closed the door.

"It is an electronic piano with earphones so we won't here anything" explained Jane. "Now what do you think of my little thesis?"

"The Prof told me that the words you have written are one thing but hearing you go through it is something else so give me something else!"

"Let us hope he is as right as he usually is. All this started when Catherine took notes and you had gone through various points and said you would reiterate them provided you could remember them all and Catherine had written it down and offered you a print. Well the Prof had another printer in his kitchen and I read that when it suddenly spewed out the discussion points. Having thought abut things I made a couple of suggestions and was delighted that they were taken up. It whetted my appetite. I used to drool over the shear delight of being in the Space service but with marriage and children and so on that side of my nature had been quiet. I just started musing over some of the things that have been said and don't forget I have been helping Catherine Whistler out in the archiving. Well that meant I got to see and read everything that was going on and there were a few loose ends so to speak.

I am sure you must have concluded that with our use of the rethe for jumps we could cut away or we could add time on. Mathematically we could compress or stretch it but we could never go through it.

With your studies of Sonny and FB1 you almost spoke of something that was obviously in your semi sub conscious mind without actually going that final step. It suddenly occurred to me that we are dealing here with the infinite and that a new branch of mathematics may develop as we try to explain what our theories predict. When you look at a computor tree you may see a folder titled 'my photos' and you may also see the same title appearing in different parts of the tree. There are not two folders but you can access the same folder from a different route. I started to see the rethe as a dividing line between our world and the negative world with access through except that we have never yet been through we have stopped in no mans land, namely the rethe. It struck me that in the existence of negative matter, time may well also have a negative value and if we could access it possibly we could go back or forwards in time. I started to see the rethe as the boundary between the positive existence and the negative existence. There will no doubt be laws of physics that govern all of this and the dividing line between the two existences is the rethe. I feel sure that the inverse time law is generated as the two systems rub up against each other. To us the rethe seems vast but in the infinities it is of course small. The line between existencies which we have termed the rethe is not perfect. Near but not quite. Every so often there is a bubble containing a half and half mix such as Sonny or FB1. The reason that the rethe exhibits a zero time dimension is that it is equally influenced by our side and the other side. The only way you will be able to get into the other side is via something akin to FB1. You have to go through it and because of that time travel is impossible! However another thought struck me and that was that not only can we access the rethe, but entities from the other side can also do that. If we were both in the rethe together an exchange may be possible, provided we could guarantee the exact same mass.

Now when we exit and enter the rethe we do it by means of enveloping ourselves in a cocoon. That cocoon obviously has the properties to eject us back to whence we came, but if its properties could be influenced we may be able to make it eject us on the negative side and so we would then be possibly into the true realm of time travel."

Jane drew breath and noticed that the Whistler was into his robot trance again and she sat back and watched his eyelids flickering just as if he was in a dream. After about five minutes or so he resurfaced and said "The Prof was not wrong. You really do have a way of putting the flesh onto the bones. Jane, there are that many avenues opening up from those ideas I really don't know where we should start!"

"How about starting with a cup of tea?"

"That funny British habit does somehow provide start and finish points doesn't it?"

They went into the other room and were met with a grinning Captain Johnson who was 'dancing' to tunes being played by Josie but all in silence due to the quality of the head phones.

Jane went through into the kitchen and plugged the kettle in. Five minutes later she wheeled an old fashioned hostess trolley out with a teapot, a jug of milk and some sugar together with a selection of biscuits.

"Well what do you think of her thesis then?" asked Kingdom.

The Whistler rocked back in his chair and said "Kingdom, I have just received the biggest workload of my career. Her ideas surely have hit a target exactly in the middle. I will discuss things with Helen and I do believe that we need a branch of maths capable of operating in the world of infinites. That alone will tax the best minds in the world! She suggested with impeccable logic and intuition that we have only one sure-fire way to get to the anticlockwise zone, as she puts it, and that is to dive into Sonny and somehow come out the other side. I don't think that we can do that but I am sure she is right in that it provides a link. Whilst under her spell it occurred to me that we might reorientate FB1 and put it into the rethe again then send an unmanned ship in with it and see if it can dive through so to speak. Jane suffered a sudden sharp intake of breath as she considered the Whistler's notion and over the next five minutes she would occasionally nod in the affirmative. Finally she smiled.

Josie observed "You are almost as bad as James you know!" after that the evening became purely social and Josie Whistler was still to come to terms with the fact that although she was a cleaning lady she was sitting here in very cosy comfort with the two most powerful men involved in Space research. Life can be strange she thought as she recalled vividly how she had spotted Captain Johnson in female form as Helen had taken her place on the dais.

Just before the Whistlers went home Jane took James to one side and said "you know the Space archiving system is a valuable research tool. Grandad may have invented the original system and lord knows that was complex enough but Catherine has had to modify it bit by bit to cope with the ever increasing load. I would never have been able to come up with my load of twaddle if it wasn't for Catherine and her system!"

"I think you must now take a salary let's say similar to Catherine's, but you would be the archive research guru. Have you been doing all this work gratis?"

"Well I have and I am glad to have done it just to help Catherine out, but now you mention it a bit of pocket money would not go amiss!"

"Ok you can look in the mail in a few days time and there will be an offer for you. I only expected to get married I didn't expect this massive shift in the way we do things!"

He took Josie's arm and they went off together waving as their car lurched off down the road.

"What was that little aside there squirt?" asked Kingdom.

"I've just been offered a job without me having to do anything extra."

"Is that really so?" said the cap as they went inside.

CHAPTER 16

SECURITY ISSUES

The Whistler had called a board meeting and as he called it to order he made it known that though there would of course always be an 'any other business' section the prime purpose of this meeting was to establish security.

One of the hawks immediately spat out "another useless waste of money!"

James Whistler drew breath but Jarvis Kellar fixed the hawk with a look of fury and said "when any employee of this company receives death threats from the mob it will, it *will, WILL BE TAKEN SERIOUSLY*!"

The hawk that represented the financial institutions involved in part financing the Space administration simply sneered. "So who has been threatened with death then?"

"As a matter of fact, I have and not only that have any of you ever heard of Jane Johnson?"

One member of the board offered "isn't she the one who saw first extra terrestrial life?"

"Indeed she is, you have remembered from the last big board meeting, and she was also the architect of the methodology employed on the last Space mission. Frankly your knowledge is such that most of you do not deserve a position on this board!" She has also not only been threatened but only avoided kidnapping by the skin of her teeth and that by suggestions and actions taken not emanating from this board" as Jarvis Kellar finished speaking the hawk was not cowed or even bothered by these revelations.

The Whistler spoke quietly, "Thank you Jarvis, I now invite the board to listen to proposals put by those I would like to see in charge of security. He nodded and his PA invited the Ford brothers into the room. Both wore identical suits and looked every inch like polished business men.

"These men are Don and Peter Ford. Peter has the requisite Space travel experience and Don has experience of running some large departments in organisations. Gentlemen the Ford brothers have the floor."

Peter Ford stood up and said "firstly we offer our personal files for scrutiny by you all. I was caught up in the Mule scandal and my brother Don here was similarly caught up in the Donkey scandal that followed. We both found ourselves on the wrong side of the fence and owe our extrication from dire circumstances to some members of the Space service only one of whom do we see here" he nodded at the Whistler.

"Don rescued Jane Johnson from the clutches of the mob. She required intervention of a most forceful type, and the same may be required for each of you. We have done some research using our old contacts and we would be pleased to hear explanations of behaviour from you Mr. Flannery."

"Me?" Stuttered our erstwhile hawk.

"Yes, you!" said Don from the opposite side of the table. "It appears that you have mob money behind you!"

Flannery tried to bluster his way out of it but Peter Ford gave out copies to each other person in the room and said "explain that!"

Flannery had gone red with anger as he realised that the Ford's had got hold of his bank statements.

"We are waiting Mr. Flannery!" smiled Jarvis Kellar.

"I am not going to be insulted like this I am off!" and he stood up to go only to find his way barred by a couple of burly police officers, one of whom was already reading the arrest warrant and advising him of his rights.

Don Ford then grinned and said "I think that matter is at a close. Now having demonstrated our efficiency to you, perhaps you would like to peruse our documents," and he proffered these to the Whistler and then to each of the others. James Whistler perused the documents carefully finally raising his eyebrows and sniffing loudly.

"This is a lot of money so I suggest an alternative amount, I think we should double it, furthermore I think you should both have a seat on this board and I think part of your remunerative package should be a share option. How does that sound?"

"That sounds like the Prof talking to me!" said Fordy. "We have opened up a bank account in the name shown on the reverse of sheet four please make payments in advance each month into that account!" Only the Whistler had a sheet four and he noted with an inner smile that the account was in the name of Grontlewich Enterprises Ltd.

"Gentlemen, as you know our organisation is unusual in that though I have a board of directors full executive power is invested in me. I accept the costs as proposed by our security advisors, with my suggestions as an addendum. Are there any objections?"

"Not an objection, but may I see the cost implications please?" asked Jarvis Kellar. The Whistler rose from his chair and took sheet four. Jarvis Kellar read it and nodded.

The meeting was called to a close but one other director asked about the two directors who had resigned a few weeks ago.

"We invited Mr. Elliman to go away and he has done just that, Mr. Schweitzer is under direct scrutiny as we speak", replied Peter Ford.

The questioner admitted that he was out of his depth in such matters and grinned that he was pleased that there was someone who was able to take care of such things. Don Ford gave out business cards to each departing member.

As the room emptied leaving just the Space admin guys and the Ford brothers, James Whistler grinned and slapped Don Ford on the back saying "Christ you've had a busy couple of days!"

Fordy smiled back saying "Not half we haven't; the resistance cells still meet you know and very few folk know of more than one cell, but I do of course and it is these wallahs that we know we can trust, we will maintain the cellular structure of the resistance for our own security purpose. We have tails on the guys that we suspect at the moment. Remembering the speed with which the Donkey in particular spread his influence we will have to be extremely vigilant. Thanks for the money it will be well spent we can say that to you with confidence. I have read some of the notes from the archives and now I know why the mule failed. He failed through lack of thoroughness; Captain Johnson even put himself, you and the Prof through the mincer while he was trying to elicit who he was up against. That sort of dedication will be needed again; we are going to have to vet any one and every one in senior and junior positions.

"Agreed!" said the Whistler.

Over the coming month all senior posts were vetted and Josie Whistler volunteered to be checked out.

Don Ford sucked on his bottom teeth and said "yes we aren't finished until the spouse/girlfriend links have been checked out!"

When Don Ford went to the Johnson's to check them out Jane wouldn't let him start until she had thanked him for saving her life and given him a cup of coffee.

"Bribery will get you nowhere!" he said. He asked very personal and insulting questions to them both and had the satisfaction of seeing one of Captain Johnson's eyebrows raise, and Jane Johnson was just about to explode.

"Ok, I am as I expected to be, fully satisfied and I still don't think what I asked was as direct or as shocking as what you asked the Prof!"

Kingdom Johnson nodded in agreement saying, "That was the hardest thing I ever had to do and yet that old man simply held my gaze and stated that he was not involved in running a vicious Space empire in his spare time! I candidly admit that whatever my face showed I found that interview bruising."

Fordy relaxed and said "well I owe, no me and my brother, we owe you everything. You told me that you recognised a spark of decency in me that had hitherto not been allowed to flourish, and even if that was just politics talking, it tipped the balance of my beliefs. I have never had chance to thank you properly for that so here is a bottle of Space lubricant!"

"Oooooh! Only the blue label!" exclaimed Jane, you won't be taking that up there with you I can tell you that!"

"How is Peter doing bye the way?"

"Well as you know my background is paramilitary but Peter's is more organisational. He seems to have a second sense of what moves other organisations will make and we have so far been able to nip things in the bud. No doubt the mob will reorganise themselves but for the moment we have the upper hand.

"When we do Eric Whistler" said Fordy, "we would like to do it together as my brother has something to say".

Fast forward twenty four hours and the junior Whistlers welcomed the Ford brothers into their home. Peter Ford came straight to the point.

"Please Mr. Whistler; give it me straight, did you actually know how many people had been offered high positions in mule society?"

Eric Whistler held his face implacable for a full minute before he conceded that it had been an inspired guess.

"Perhaps it was more inspired than you know. Within seconds of you making that pronouncement, word of it reached the Mule and he was distraught. I found that out from another prisoner on Titan. As for myself I thought it might have been a clever ploy. I am quite chuffed to find out I was right!"

"Yes we were right up against it at the time, and we needed something to shock the new order wallahs. I concede now that it would have been a criminal folly to have wasted a man such as yourself, and I do not wish to be placed in such a position again!"

Peter Ford proffered his hand and Eric Whistler smiled and shook it. "It was me who told Don that you were alive and well on Titan."

"Life on Titan was not that bad and I heard that some of the old spin and bullshit politicians have been sent there. Should there be a mission in that direction I volunteer to be part of it, in fact if the date of such a mission could be adjusted we could go there for sports day!"

Eric Whistler of course knew of the gliding competitions and said "I will put it to James Whistler, but more than that I can not do. Let's just hope that he likes the idea as much as I do."

The question and answer session then began and the Fords successfully upset both Catherine and Eric. Catherine rounded on them with such spirit that both men flinched.

"God I'll be glad when this part of our operation is over! Ok you are as we expected cleaner than an operating theatre.

We both thank you for the part you played in straightening us out so perhaps you would accept this as a token of our gratitude."

"Blue label" grinned Catherine as she grabbed the bottle. "This is for our cabinet unless anyone would like a glass just now?"

Four small glasses clinked and a quick swig was enjoyed.

"Have you got girl friends?" enquired Eric, "because they will need to be grilled."

"We have and mine goes back to before mule days said Peter, but Don's is a recent addition."

"Having just witnessed me killing her old boss I don't think it would be humane to grill Imelda" said Don, "can we let her off after all she did call the police exactly as I asked her to?"

"You are running the show! observed Eric.

The Fords knew that to gain full credence they would have to brace themselves, and to their credit they did it. To coin a phrase Imelda went apeshit. She rained blows down on Fordy until her strength gave out then fell onto him sobbing.

Fordy was impressed by her attitude and told her so once she had calmed down, and he knew she was as straight as they come. Peter's girl was simply mystified by the nature of the questions, and basically couldn't really answer any of them. The two women were pronounced clean.

The Svenssons were next on the list and it fell to Peter Ford to do the honours.

Again he found the severity of the questions distasteful and the Svenssons found it even worse. Finally Peter let it be known that they were as he expected as clean as a new pin.

Peter Ford admitted that he had just begun to have doubts about the new order when circumstances dictated that he was to be ejected into Space.

"The inside of my space suit needed a thorough valleting I don't mind admitting. But strangely my time on Titan healed me and I was elected chairman- me! Perhaps you would accept this token from me and Don. He offered the bottle.

Helen grabbed it "Only blue label" she grinned. "That is for special guests only!" she said putting the bottle away. She turned from her drinks cabinet to find two grinning men looking expectantly at her. "Oh alright then, just the one!" and she poured three glasses out.

The Ford brothers quickly went through all of top men including the Whistler, the Prof and the Judds.

The toughest going was against Helen when she was at work on her own. She fired questions back at them as the interview proceeded and suddenly Fordy laughed outright. "I don't know if that was official or not but we have just been grilled. You are a clever lady!" Helen asked them a few more questions and these seemed to satisfy her so she offered them both a machine coffee.

"No it was not official, but I was almost conscripted into the mule's network and no-one is going to catch me out again. You two boys do appear to be clean!"

She held out her hand.

"What's that for?" asked Fordy. "The bottles!" she grinned. They each gave her a bottle of blue label, and without hesitation she opened one and poured it into the coffees.

"I always wanted to waste something precious" she smiled.

Her door opened and James Whistler poked his head in and asked for the results of the interview. "Oh they're clean" Helen smirked. "Fancy a drop of earth lubricant?"

James Whistler came in with his coffee and protested as Helen offered to pour blue label into the coffee. "Go on live a little!" with that the three men roared with laughter. Helen was the only one that the Fords interviewed twice, and she wasn't sure why they had decided to do that, but she had taken the opportunity to quietly grill them and Fordy had suddenly realised what she was doing. She was confident in their ability and quite convinced of their straightness. The reason that she had been done twice was that she held a powerful position in her own right but she also had the spouse link and after much heart-searching the Fords had decided she could do with an extra grilling. This would also set a precedent should similar circumstances reoccur. Although the questions they asked were highly personal and cleverly designed they went about it in as pleasant a manner as was possible and both men were of a garrulous nature. Helen, realising this had used questions in her answers and the Ford brothers replied to the questions though after about six or so Fordy had realised how cleverly she had manipulated them.

Captain Johnson's first reaction on hearing of her double grilling was a flash of anger but then he grinned widely saying "That's my girl!" when he heard how she had dealt with it. When he had time to reflect he realised that the Ford brothers were leaving nothing to chance and his original angry reaction was replaced by satisfaction.

During the next week or so the 'new security' as they badged themselves installed panic buttons in the cars of the top wallahs and their wives. This was a just in case move as the Fords knew that the mob would be looking for any weak link in defences. The mob was no where near as powerful as pre-reformation days, but still were an unfortunate fact of life. All gardens were given anti prowler surveillance just in case and this resulted in the arrest of a few youths, who were simply going where they shouldn't go.

James Whistler felt his confidence rising and asked the Fords to give Mr. Schweitzer a long leash whilst monitoring him carefully. He then felt able to focus his mind on Jane's latest notions. Jane was no mathematician but yet she had grasped the notion of introduction of a factor to explain the unexplainable. He and Helen made great inroads into explaining the actions of the negative or anticlockwise world, successfully applying Newton's laws to most things but of course there was no way of proving any thing.

CHAPTER 17

THE WHISTLER STRETCHES HIS MIND

They tried to bring equations to bear on the infinite. Now this was a non starter and though he could see why Jane had conceived that notion, he realised that you couldn't manipulate infinites in normal equations, and yet some where at the back of his mind was the idea of having infinite quantities modified by finite quantities. He couldn't rid his mind of the idea of infinity divided by infinity as being equal to unity or one. Was infinity squared a higher value than infinity itself? So somehow there had to be a means of manipulating very big things. Perhaps something that was virtual-infinite. That is to say so large as to appear infinite yet not quite so possessed of properties to render it un-manipulable. He decided to think about this over night or as it turned out several nights.

He dreamt of Space and the Solar system, he dreamt of Stellar 2 and that system he dreamt of the huge distance between to two galaxies, and he dreamt of what lay beyond. If this was finite then what? Somehow, the finite and the infinite lived cheek by jowl. Perhaps there was no such thing as infinite. Perhaps infinity was something with no perceived boundary. After all a circle was just that, you could roll round the circumference for ever and yet the circle was bounded by the finite.

Each morning he awoke feeling more tired than when he went to bed. It was wearing him out.

He considered life. Now this was most definitely finite and yet the notion of life propagation was infinite.

He dreamt on.

When he awoke on the fourth morning he didn't feel so tired. As he lay there thinking, Josie turned and said "Well what all this about a tesseract, and what the hell is one then?"

"Maybe the answer to my prayers! But in answer to your question, we have a point, a straight line, a square, a cube and next, is a tesseract."

"Hmmmm!"

Later that day at work James Whistler made his usual early morning visit to Helen's office. She took one look at him and said "you've cracked it!"

"I am a long way from that but I was thinking about real and imaginary numbers using the j operator. Every decent engineer knows about them. Then I thought of the four dimensional tesseract and I wonder whether or not we could invent a multi dimensional shape which we could call a sexteract or an octocube perhaps. We could ascribe infinite values or at least semi infinite values to an axis inside our shape and use the other axes to quantify relationships of known finite quantities. Helen looked intrigued. "I suppose the idea here is to have axes for our three dimensions and another three for similar negative world dimensions and two infinite ones for time, one for our time and one for the other time the anticlockwise time!"

"That's the general idea!" he smiled and continued to expound his thesis to Helen. "Perhaps we could introduce the 'v' operator, where 'v' stands for vast, or in effect partially infinite!"

Note from Catherine Whistler. Don't worry I couldn't begin to describe the meaning of the discussions that followed. Both Jane Johnson and I are mystified by the concept, so I will not attempt further explanation as I am past the limit of my knowledge. I only know that after weeks, and then months of further study the Space service was ready for another step forward.

CHAPTER 18

A REVIEW OF THE SITUATION AND A NEW FACE

The Whistler and Helen had entered into a full collaboration on the maths involved for their project. It had been mind blowingly difficult but they had basically conceived a new branch of mathematics and were now confident of their thesis.

They invited the Prof to be their master of ceremonies as they toured the major seats of learning to express them selves and to see how the ideas went down.

The Prof still had his magic touch and he used a small amount of good humour which somehow the audiences became infected with, and there was almost no heckling.

The concepts were so much into the mathematician's world that the press basically left them alone, as few reporters could make sense of this notion.

The Whistler always started with the same line which went---'I am not Einstein, though sometimes I wish I were'---. After the lecture questions from the floor were thick and varied and in essence were a searching review of the thesis.

At one lecture one young man stood after the lecture and asked a few questions. The Whistler found that these questions had a tenor to them that showed the questioner had a surprisingly good grasp of the maths, better than any other questioner.

"Mr. Whistler, I know you are a scientist of some note so when an engineer like myself asks you some questions, they are based upon engineering rather than science. I have an overburdening curiosity to know what the drive behind your thesis is, as I feel sure it is something to do with time travel. Am I right?"

The Whistler grinned and invited the questioner to come and see him after the lecture was over. Half an hour later the young man made his way to the dais as others were exiting the hall.

Firstly he grabbed the Prof's hand and shaking it enthusiastically introduced himself.

"Hello Prof, I have wanted to meet you since I was a little boy. My name is Smedley Tomlinson!"

The Prof returned the enthusiasm in his own hand shake, and said "Well, Smedley, I must introduce Mr. James Whistler."

Smedley rushed headlong into his own life story and said "when you had theories, I remember that professor Trueblood trying to discredit you and nearly all of my fellow students pooh-poohed your ideas and backed Trueblood. I championed your ideas and actually made myself a little bit unpopular. It got worse when you turned out to be correct! I did write to the Space authorities asking for an interview, but I think my letter may have gone with everything else the Donkey did, down the pan!"

The Whistler stood and gazed at Smedley Tomlinson. "Perhaps your way of life is about to undergo a change, young man. The project that I am about to proceed with will have an urgent need for a top line engineer, particularly one who has a handle on advanced maths. I am not snobby about science. I know that engineering is a very close cousin and the two disciplines share much of the same philosophy. You were right in surmising that we are trying to establish a means of time travel. I think we are very close to a solution now but I must warn you that the concept will simply not allow you to travel forward and backwards over a week and thus know the lottery results before hand!" we still have about a week left on our lecture tour, you could even join in our travels with us if time permits!"

"I think my wife and daughter might get an edge grumpy if I do that" Smedley smiled. "Could I come for a job interview in say a fortnight's time at the Space administration headquarters?"

"No", said the Whistler, but you can come and take up the post I am about to offer you!" he reached for his mobile phone and enquired

Smedley's mobile number and tapped a message out. Smedley's phone rang, he read the text message and a slow flush of colour spread across his face as he gasped "I can't turn that down! I've got some explaining to do back home so I'll be off to do that. Good day gentlemen!"

James Whistler's parting shot was "You will have to undergo a thorough vetting before that offer can be finalized!"

"I look forward to that!" and Smedley Tomlinson fairly shot out of the auditorium.

The Prof and Whistler looked at each other and the Prof said "he will be ok, I can feel it!"

Helen was back at the ranch keeping things running while the lecture tour was under weigh and she was immediately curious to meet Smedley Tomlinson when the Whistler told her what he had done.

"I knew we needed a top line man as soon as our theory looked like it would hold water, because I know our present Space ships will be useless for time travel. I was wondering where we would find someone with a grasp of the maths who was also an engineer," she marvelled.

Three weeks later Smedley and his wife had emerged from the vetting and were pronounced clean. Kay Tomlinson muttered something about finding out the true meaning of the word 'thorough' and had found herself sweating under the relentless pressure of the questions.

Even Smedley had found that the Ford brothers had discovered little things about him that he had almost forgotten himself. He had been given an office two doors down from Helen's office and when he had first made her acquaintance he called her 'Mrs. Svensson.'

"Well I'm going to call you 'Smedley' Mr. Tomlinson, but you can please yourself!"

"I do rather like the name 'Helen' you know, in fact it is my daughter's middle name. She is Rebecca Helen Tomlinson."

Smedley's reputation as an engineer spread quickly as he repaired one or two faulty laptops and showed he was also good with his hands. He made a small wooden model of the Freeloader and considering he had only seen press releases of it, it was a very close likeness.

Some one looked at his model which had found its way to a cabinet in the canteen and said "Who's made that?" the vernacular reply since he was sitting in there was "He's med it!" and shortly thereafter his nickname derived from that short reply was 'Smed'.

The Whistler was delighted that his protégé had so quickly become part of the furniture so to speak.

He was given a month to settle in and then the Whistler gave him something to chew on. He went through all of the theorising about the anticlockwise world and our clockwise world basically sandwiching the rethe, and how the notion was that time had a reverse vector the other side of the rethe. He then came to the one major stumbling block that had been encountered and that they could not see any way of going into the rethe and coming out on the other side. The Whistler was certain that there would be a way but it would take those with a practical turn of mind to crack the issue hence his need for an engineer.

"You don't want much then!" chuckled Smed, resignedly.

That evening at home he told his wife of the task that lay before him. She had had a hard day as their daughter had been fractious, so she only half listened. Two hours later she suddenly said "What exactly do they want you to do?"

He explained his task in lay terms as best as he was able. "They won't ask you to go first will they?" she worried.

"Actually Kay, I am part of a team, there really doesn't seem to be an 'us and them' mentality but in answer to your question I think any such mission must be unmanned at least initially, but that raises enough issues on its own to occupy a good engineer for half his lifetime!"

As it turned out he would find one shard of the solution window a lot sooner than that.

He had watched the TV the day Catherine Whistler had reduced the abrasive nitwit to a gibbering wreck and enquired if there was a copy of her books within the Space library. He was given Catherine's phone number.

He rang without delay and Catherine realised who it was before he had introduced himself.

"Ah, the new kid on the block!" she said. He then did formally introduce himself and asked if he could avail himself of a copy of her books.

"You will be in the next one in all probability!" she laughed. "Actually I think Helen may have her copy, I think if you ask she will be able to lay her hands on it!"

He had felt himself a little in awe as that TV interview had given her a strong notoriety but he warmed to her and realised she must have been very pressed to let fly as she had done on that interview. Ok Mrs. Whistler I will no doubt speak to you again. Thanks for your help. Bye!"

"Bye and its Catherine to you, Smed!"

The last thing he heard before the phone cut off was her chuckling.

He had heard of her books but more importantly he remembered Captain Johnson being interviewed on TV saying that anyone who wanted to know of the personalities involved could do no better than to read the books. He read both books twice. He had been blessed from birth with a very retentive memory and he could understand that Grandad then Catherine had done a first class job in bringing the basics of the engineering to the attention of the reading public.

His engineering mind had a ready grasp of new concepts and he quickly realised that the gravity motor mark 2 was the key to achieving anything like the speed required to make a jump into the rethe. He considered the gravity motor mark 2 and how it had developed and the germ of an idea took root at the back of his mind.

He asked the Whistler for his opinion on what would happen if the gravity motor on its own with no attendant spaceship to drag after it would do if it went into the rethe.

The Whistler thought long and hard about this and concluded that since it was not subject to gravitational pull, it would not be subject to many of the forces being applied to positive matter, and this if somehow it was moved against the walls of the rethe cocoon there was no way of knowing what reaction the cocoon wall may have.

"Ok" said Smed "if we made two such gravity motors one surrounding positive matter and one surrounding negative matter if the negative matter one was open when we try to exit the rethe, do you think it would come out on the other side?"

The Whistler drew an excited breath "My god you could be right!" he exclaimed "But where do we get the piece of negative matter from?" he frowned.

"Sonny or FB1" came the quick reply.

"Smed, I think you have earned a place for your wife and youngster at a party at the Prof's place!"

"What parties are those then?" asked Smed in all innocence.

"At the height of his career the Prof was number two to Captain Johnson and he has a remarkably sophisticated mind. He has spotted things I would never have spotted in a thousand years, and he has a son now known as Judder, who has an almost identical ability. If we put your idea to them and it is right they will spot in an instant that it is and they will spot danger zones as well!" Nearly all of the advancements made in the last few years have resulted from discussions at his place. Sometimes the discussions are furious but they are always fruitful."

"Are they dinner jacket jobbies these parties?" enquired Smed.

"No, we all go smart casual! Now just wait a minute he looked on his computor and at his calendar then at Helen's. Ok it will be a Thursday morning 13 days from now, make sure you are available and we will travel together by glass tube train, the Prof's place is in England!"

CHAPTER 19

THE NEXT PARTY

The Tomlinson's travelled over to England with the senior Whistlers by glass tube train. Neither the Tomlinson's nor Josie Whistler had been on one before and they were amazed at the smoothness and the shear thrill of travelling at three hundred miles per hour at ground level. At that speed the tube was of necessity very straight and each curve and there were some had a very large radius. The sensation was indescribable and Rebecca in particular was grinning almost the whole of the way there. The Whistler had arranged for a chauffer driven Rolls Royce to pick them up and this marvellous old car, guzzling petrol as it went, swept them through the countryside and on the motor ways from London into Shropshire. Its tyres made glorious scrunching noises on the gravel drive at the Prof's house.

The Whistler was first out and rang the bell as he and Josie were welcomed into the house. Liz beckoned the slightly shy Tomlinsons in and soon charmed any shyness into submission.

A little voice piped up "What's your name then?"

"Rebecca!" and with that Rebecca rushed after the little boy with the striking blond hair and off into the back garden. The Prof had bought an extra piece of land that had tripled the size of his back garden and the kids were enjoying the freedom away from parental control.

Introductions were made and glasses of Martian elixir were served.

"Yes I read of that in Catherine's book, though when I had seen it on supermarket shelves I thought it was a con! admitted Smed.

"How could you think it was a con Smed?" said a voice behind him and he turned knowing he was meeting Catherine.

A couple of hours later they all sat down to a Prof meal. It was customary now for the Prof to bring in the caterers but he always did potatoes, runner beans and meat himself.

The Prof had constructed a massive garden shed and this had been done out especially for the children. They were dead chuffed and were all on their best behaviour, as their meals were served in the shed. 'The garden house' as one of them put it.

Surprisingly Kay had heard of the Prof's runner beans but Smed hadn't.

Josie Whistler chipped in "you will be the envy of the Space service if they find out you've been to one of these parties. I don't know if you've come across Heinrich Schmidt yet but he is the leading away team leader and he has only been to one of these do's, and he had wanted to come to one for years. It raises your street cred no end!"

Judder suddenly looked uncomfortable. Nadine recognised it immediately. "OK Brian spit it out, what have you done this time?"

Judder moved his head around in a circle as if trying to avoid the question but drew breath and suddenly admitted. "I have overstepped the mark. I saw Heinrich a couple of days ago and he had heard there was another party here and I simply said "see you there then!"

The bell rang, and the Prof was out of his chair in a flash. "Come on in Heinrich we've been expecting you!"

There was a sudden ripple of laughter as the assemblage knew that Mr. Judd had been expertly unpickled by his dad.

Judder mouthed thanks to his dad as Heinrich was given the customary Martian elixir.

Nadine grinned in shear delight as she recognised the elegance of the Prof's move to allay any embarrassment that may have been caused. "What a cracking old guy!" she thought.

After the meal Heinrich wandered across and bade good evening to Captain Johnson who introduced Smed. "Everybody in the Space admin knows of Smed!" said Heinrich.

Kingdom Johnson smiled and said "well you've got a head start so all you've got to do is to avoid blotting your copybook!"

Smed was slightly nervous when he replied "tell what you think after tomorrow!"

Kingdom Johnson replied, "I'll tell you what I think now. In the Space research we are always only inches away from finding things we can't explain. And if we can't that's ok. The only thing that we abhor is bullshit. We just stick to plain fact."

In spite of his worries Smed wiped his brow and grinned "thank god for that. Bullshit is my second worst subject; I think Kay will tell you that romance is my worst!"

Heinrich and Kingdom laughed outright. "He will make it!" said Heinrich as Smed wandered off in search of his wife.

The women had at this point all congregated over in a corner and Kay who liked to read the gossip columns said well I heard that you all sang 'What a' as the others joined in with 'swell party this is!'

Kay burst into a peal of laughter "So it is true then!"

Just then little Rebecca rushed into the arms of her advancing father and said "daddy I am tired!"

Kay and Smed both looked guilty as neither had even considered sleeping.

"Hannah Jackson came across and took the normally shy Rebecca in her arms saying "well let's see what we can do about that then!"

Hannah always had that kindly image that children recognised in an instant and she carried Rebecca out to the 'garden house'. Quite a number of the children had fallen asleep and as it was a warm summer evening Hannah once again found blankets and draped them over the children where they were. She found a nice corner, stood Rebecca in it and gave her a sip of orange juice and said "Not too much, we don't want a little accident do we?" Rebecca was out like a light, the moment she was wrapped in a blanket on the floor.

Hannah turned the thermostat on the wall up a little and closed the two main doors; thinking to herself what an unusual guy the Prof was in having a heated shed. She went back to where the women were still chatting.

"Hannah, how do you do that? Rebecca screams if anybody she doesn't know picks her up!"

"She's always been like that, it isn't only children but cats and dogs respond the same. I wish I had that effect on my parishioners!" boomed the sonorous voice of William Jackson. He offered his hand and Kay, like even the men found her puny little hand lost inside the huge but gentle black fist.

"Well I think that's about everybody now!" said Smed. "But where the hell are we all going to sleep, there are no hotels anywhere round here are there?"

Liz then came across and bragged in a most delightful way. "Lady Elizabeth and Sir William Wild beg to inform you that they, er we, have had an extension built and you will all find your names on the doors of the bedrooms allotted to you!" she had quietly slipped upstairs and readied a room for Heinrich, as soon as she had realised that she had got an extra guest. The Prof found words died on his lips as he was just about to remind her of Heinrich. One glance at Liz and he knew she had beaten him to the punch so to speak.

The caterers had long since cleaned away the remnants of the meal and they had also grilled plenty of bacon for the morning's breakfast.

The house fell silent as the Prof and Liz were last up the stairs.

"Beautifully bragged" smirked the Prof as Liz slid into bed beside him, "I can't wait to hear what Smed has been up to tomorrow! James has been quiet tonight, and I suppose when the other Whistlers and the Svenssons get here tomorrow our newly extended house will be absolutely full!"

They all slept well.

The next morning Kay was first up and found herself surrounded by kids all clamouring to be fed. Just as she was wondering where all the food was kept Hannah Jackson came down and smoothly took over. Kay gave as much help as she could and then slowly as the other women and Smed came down order was gradually restored. Using the bacon left by the caterers Hannah soon had every one breakfasted but just like the last time, had just got the washing up done and put away when the rest of the men straggled down.

"You'll have to feed yourselves" chorused Hannah and Kay.

"We know the form!" grinned the Prof and looking into the micro wave saw a large amount of bacon still in there. He thought he had overdone the amounts until the doorbell chimes went, and he remembered that Eric Whistler and the Svenssons were expected.

Catherine yawned a welcome to her husband, and Eric said "What's he like then?"

"Judge for yourself, he is out there playing with the kids at the moment!"

Eric helped himself to some bacon and made himself a sandwich, and watched the play in the garden. The door chimes went again and the Svensson's came in enquiring about their little boy. They caught site of him playing with the others, and sat down knowing that small relief given to parents.

Round about mid morning the Whistler rounded up all of those directly involved and they went into the Prof's study as he now called it. It was a large well lit room with a digital projector and lighting control console. All mod cons as the Prof put it.

Every one was sat facing the small pulpit and the Prof stood up. "Ladies and gentlemen, the Whistler, my good friend James offered this man a job on the spot. I think you have all met him during last night's shenanigans but if any of you didn't, I call upon Smedley Tomlinson to introduce himself. You're on son!"

Smedley stood up and scratched his head, then began. "I have only begun my career here a few short weeks ago and I am now universally known as Smed. So please use that form of address if you prefer.

If I may be so bold as to use a name known throughout the Space service: the Whistler told me that he needed a top line engineer and offered me that job. I accepted and after being grilled by the security guys I was allowed about a month to settle in during which time I uprooted my family and moved a suitable distance from my new place of employment. I really enjoyed the introductory period. Then he told me what had been his purpose in employing me.

Ok so the honeymoon period was well and truly over." He paused as a small rumble of merriment went through his audience.

"I had already studied the mathematics that he and Helen Svensson had dreamed up and being a decent mathematician myself I tried to pick holes in the theory. Now with a new branch of maths such as this there are bound to be a few rough edges but I am not good enough to find them or there aren't any. Judge for your selves where the truth lies.

Jane Johnson at the back there" he said nodding "expanded on the rethe idea expounded by Helen Svensson and caused quite a stir. So big a stir, that it spawned this new branch of maths that actually has a mechanism in it to allow manipulation of vasts. A vast is something which is infinite yet can be manipulated in equations. This branch of mathematical thought is I am sure as important as the concept of calculus.

James Whistler and Helen have just about tied up the maths relating to what used to be called the fourth dimension. They have conceived a system whereby all of the solid things that we know of can be linked via a subtle chain to the anticlockwise world surmised to be beyond the rethe. James was stuck however when it came to finding a means whereby we could get not only into and out of the rethe but through it!" He paused for the excited mumbles to die down.

"I asked James, and I know he has bounced all these ideas off Helen, what might happen if we took a piece of negative matter into the rethe. When we exited would we come out on the other side? I will say that I am not enough of a mathematician to have invented this new branch of maths but I am good enough to understand it, and I realised that with a cocoon surrounding a spaceship which is positive matter from the clockwise world, the rethe must eject the cocoon from whence it came otherwise it would upset the matter-antimatter balance. Now I wondered if we had some anti-matter and entered the rethe with it whether or not it would exit to the other side. The maths says it will. So where on earth could we possibly get some anti-matter from? We do have a couple of sources and these are Sonny and FB1. I would suggest leaving Sonny alone and concentrating our efforts on FB1.

If we can acquire some anti-matter we could enclose it with an equal mass of positive matter and so the unit would take equally from both Space time continua, and not provoke a Guy Fawkes Night.

The essence of my idea is to build a small spaceship where there are two anti gravity regions on it but around its outside. I am presuming that our gravity shield technology will be equally effective in shielding both positive and negative matter. So I propose that one motor would shield the normal matter and the other would shield the negative. Then by controlling the electro-fields around them we could activate each one individually. We would use the positive one plus some rocket power to get into the rethe then some rocket power and the other one to exit on the other side.

All of this is of course only conjecture until we can find a way to harvest some negative mass. If we can do that then we can exit the rethe into the anticlockwise world and I would suggest unmanned missions until we are confident of our technology!" he sat down to that peculiar absence of noise when no one is scarcely able to breath.

James Whistler stood and said simply "now you know why I took him on and why I have given him a reasonable salary!"

A hushed murmuring was slowly growing in volume as Smed sat down.

"How are we going to harvest negative matter?" asked Judder.

"The word was that you and the Prof might have ideas there" replied Smed. Jane here thought that the rethe is the divide between the two continua and that it is not quite perfect, having a few ragged edges resulting in the likes of FB1. If we could find another smaller one, we may be able to contain it while we do experiments, but all in all not easy!"

Helen Svensson stood and said "I am sure that Smed is right, but it may be down to us scientists to come up with some control data. If we can do that it may help Smed over this fairly big stumbling block. Everything he has said in this lecture has been accurate insofar as I can tell, and having been heavily involved in the development of the new maths I can say it all fits and we surely stand on the brink of an historic discovery!"

"Coffee any one" bawled Josie Whistler as she came in with a steaming jug. Kay and Hannah followed her in with trays of sandwiches.

"We have found an alternative means of time travel" said the Prof "after all where has the morning gone?"

They stopped for lunch; nobody noticed that Judder had been very quiet.

Judder ate his lunch and was oblivious to the lively conversations going on around him. As others wandered into the garden Judder quietly asked Smed if he had got a moment. Smed was all ears as Judder began "Smed, we mine diamond crystals from on Triton and just recently one of the mining engineers tracked down a point which seems to grow the diamond from. It has this weird property that it is not hard until some other chemical which must be a catalyst for the growth effectively evaporates away. If the diamond is forced to go down a tube as the crystal grows then we form a perfect tube of very hard substance and it can of course withstand very high temperatures. I was thinking that with a bit of ingenuity we could grow the crystal to some prescribed shape and make an exceptionally strong container with it, and I wondered if it would be strong enough to enable us to take a slug out of the middle of FB1 and come out with both sorts of matter inside it. We could then super cool it and I hope that the two matters would slowly become less active and each would condense into a globule, and then we would have an amount of matter and an exactly equal amount of anti-matter. What do you think?"

"Christ I can understand why you are where you are Judder that sounds a real possibility, let's go and bend the Whistler's ear for a few moments!"

James Whistler listened carefully and his face flickered between one of intense concentration and his robotic expression.

He suddenly stood and called every one back to the lecture room. "I think two of our resident genii have just shown the value of a working lunch." James Whistler called Judder to speak and Judder obliged.

Suddenly the notion of getting some negative matter began to sound practical, particularly as the acquisition would be an unmanned mission. The Whistler realised that much would depend on the ability to grow diamond crystals to a shape where thrusting the tube into the heart of FB1 and forcing a slug of material into the tube to an exact amount would depend on some tricky engineering. The tubes would have to be sealed at both ends but with a flap valve or some device to allow the ingress of material, but with a gas tight seal to keep it all in.

The Whistler immediately called for growing experiments to be conducted on Triton and put Judder in charge of that. The sealing of the tube was left to Smed. And he decided to use stainless steel as his modelling clay, with a promise to get on with his ideas immediately. The Whistler decided that Helen and he himself would try to crack the problem of how much material they needed and whether there was a natural force they could harness to help with the harvesting.

The Prof glowed as he realised that Judder may well have turned a key in one of the final locks in this human struggle.

Finally the Prof cracked open his bottle of blue label and offered small glasses all round. The rest of the day was spent with people pondering and rejecting a whole fistful of fanciful ideas.

There was an enlightened intellectual buzz about the place when the phone rang and the Prof returned with a very grave look on his face.

"Gentlemen we are being bugged. That was Fordy and already he has found out that the mob is puzzling over our meeting this afternoon. Eric Whistler produced his bug pen and went all round the lecture room finding nothing he then turned the pen onto himself and found nothing. The first sign of a problem was the reverend. The pen beeped loudly. William Jackson took his jacket off and the beeping revealed a bug in the lining of his jacket. Eric removed the battery from it then checked everyone else including the children and found nothing more.

William Jackson wondered how a bug could have been planted and Hannah supplied the answer. "I took that jacket to the cleaners and only got it back yesterday. I shall go and give them a piece of my mind!"

"Hannah much as I would love to go with you whilst you chew up some probably innocent youngster, I think we should leave this to the professionals" frowned the Prof.

"I beg you to remember, reverend, these folk have no conscience they profess to be catholic but their only allegiances are to money and fear. They use the one to make the other," murmured the Prof "These insects are beginning to annoy me!"

It went quiet for a few moments but the Prof said "I have just invited our security wallahs here and they have asked if you would be so kind as to hang on for a while."

Half an hour later Fordy came in with his face covered with a plastic mask looking like a caricature of the latest heartthrob film star.

Fordy grinned as he removed the mask and opened a briefcase full of electronic stuff. The partygoers all looked on with interest as Fordy switched something on and finger across lips wrote on paper for the Prof "YOUR PHONE IS BUGGED". He reached into the little case and fetched out a small disc player and set it to play music then placed it by the hall phone. Fordy relaxed and asked who else had been in the house. "Only the caterers!" said Liz. Fordy then indicated that every persons phone be checked and asked if anyone had a faulty phone. Kay said "I can hardly get the lid onto mine!"

Fordy had a look and found a new phone battery from his case of parts and put this into Kay's phone. He checked it was functional and then looked at the battery he had removed, it had been tampered with, but this was not noticeable unless you were studying it carefully.

He asked the Prof to phone for enough cabs to take every one home then thought again and doubled the number of cabs. He then instructed everyone to get home as quickly as possible. Some cabs left empty and some were full but in the dark it was impossible to tell which were which and within half an hour he had despatched every one but remained himself advising the Prof that he may get visitors during the night.

The Prof left one window unlocked and then put a few trip obstacles along his hall and landing and went to bed. Fordy loved these games and yet he didn't really think of himself as a hard man.

He was though and he was rewarded at about three am when a moonlit shadow flitted across one of the windows, he heard handles being quietly tried and finally the intruders, there were three entered the house. Fordy had a set of night vision goggles and the latest ones were not too cumbersome being only slightly heavier that a good pair of sunglasses. He silently stepped behind the first man and hit him a ferocious blow on the back of the neck. He went down loudly.

"Christ shhhhh!" came a whisper. This man grunted as the drug dart hit him and he sank more slowly. Fordy placed his empty dart gun down and readied his pistol slipping the safety catch off just as he hit the lights the third man spun and lunged but Fordy caught him on the temple with his pistol and he went down. Fordy had a number of long nylon ties in his pocket and he bound each man up with them switching the light off and he slipped out to go and check on the driver. This man was sitting in the car yawning. He resumed full consciousness the moment Fordy's pistol stuck in his neck. Fordy flicked open his own mobile phone and snarled "your cover is blown!" as he photographed the guy. He pulled the gun away from the driver's neck still snarling "now piss off!" The car roared off down the drive and away into the distance. Fordy scouted round the extremes of the property and even with his night glasses on saw nothing more. He dialled a number. "Three" he said. Shortly an ambulance arrived and three bodies were loaded in for questioning. Fordy left and the Prof slept on.

Two days later the Prof was both angry and surprised that Fordy had had to immobilise three thugs, and he realised that the mob would be after world domination if it wasn't stopped.

He ruminated that democracy was such a delicate thing, but without a bit of steel, it would be like a grape starved of water, it would wither on the vine. He rang Fordy and asked if he could help.

CHAPTER 20

SECURITY ISSUES

Fordy was delighted to hear from him and he asked if the Prof could help sifting through the steadily growing amount of personal data. The Prof agreed and sat and read for hours as he printed out the succession of e-mails that began to arrive. Part way through the sifting a pattern emerged and the Prof grimly realised that James Whistler had underestimated Mr. Schweitzer. The Prof advised Fordy of his suspicions.

Fordy sucked on his teeth and checked in to the attendance record and since the virtual disappearance of Mr. Elliman; Mr. Schweitzer had been spending a great deal more time at the Space centre. The man was a hawk, but that was just the outward face presented to the world, in fact he was a highly intelligent man who had started like many others at the bottom, then diverging from the norm he cultivated the wrong contacts as he worked his way steadily down into the underworld. His car veered off the road and went over a cliff on a coastal road during his next break. He was alone in the vehicle. The crash did not kill him as the death certificate showed he had died of exposure.

The inquest added a rider that for reasons unknown he had not managed to use his mobile phone which was still operational as with help he would certainly have survived.

The Prof read of this on an internet news page and grimly smiled as he thought this was a showing of the little bit of steel so sorely needed.

Fordy, his brother and the Prof all worked diligently and the Prof's peculiar humanistic ability made him suspect people including one of the cleaning ladies who was a friend of Josie. When questioned she denied all knowledge of any wrongdoing.

Fordy was not only aggressive, he was clever and subtle and he conned her into an admission at which point she broke down.

Fordy gave Josie Whistler a prepared script and asked her to learn it fully, thereafter he sent Josie round to the cleaning lady's home.

Josie had known this woman for some time and was shocked to learn of her duplicity. She used Fordy's script intelligently and found that her friend's son was at university and his life had been threatened by the mob. The threat had been issued by Mr. Schweitzer, and he had been her contact.

Fordy mulled this over and asked Peter for his opinion, then asked the Prof. Their agreed view was to leave the woman in place and try to find out who exactly was likely to despatch her son. Then wait until someone else contacted her. She was caught between the devil and the deep but knew her life would be a torment for ever unless she could remove the threat to her family and she agreed to cooperate but with immense trepidation.

Note from Catherine Whistler. I shall refer to this woman as Jessica but that is not her real name. The influence and fear engendered by the activity of the mob makes this essential, she is more relaxed about it these days but still believes the mob is out to get her.

About three weeks later Jessica found a hand written note pushed through her letterbox. She feared the worst as she read it, but it was from Fordy saying that the immediate threat to her son's life had been removed and he had agreed to continue his studies at another university, under another name.

She felt extremely grateful and fearful at the same time. She burned the letter and awaited developments. About a week later another of the cleaning ladies made an oblique threat of a personal nature. Jessica was perceptive enough to realise that this new threat was from the mob, so she told Josie Whistler.

Perhaps Josie had been a man in a former life, because her reaction was to go straight round and give a savage physical beating to the woman. The woman spat blood from her mouth and told Josie she may have won the fight but there were thousands like her ready to take up the cause. Josie called the New Security chaps who took the woman away for questioning, and Josie wondered how anyone could be that misguided.

Peter Ford let the Whistler know that Josie had raised her profile by her act and had increased the general personal danger level. He also said if there were a few more like her then the whole security system would be tighter.

Perhaps the one thing that the mob was unaccustomed to dealing with was that their target was quite willing to play dirty. Amongst themselves there had been many vicious power struggles, but they had been able to rely on the authorities appearing to seem scrupulously playing within the law, hog tying themselves in the process. Right now however was during the early part of the reformation and the authorities were not quite so hog tied as previously.

One of the resistance cells reported that a quiet and well respected family had been observed and these folk who still lived a luxurious lifestyle seemed to have a number of known hoodlums meet with them. More than would be expected if they were suffering threats.

Peter Ford ordered that a careful watch be kept over a few weeks to ascertain the likely truth of the allegation. After about a fortnight he convinced Don that this family were effectively godfathers. Fordy used his own contacts to check out the situation, and finally conceded that Peter was correct. The villa stood on a hill top and was surrounded by high stone walls with only one road leading up there so a surreptitious approach was near impossible. The only vehicle with a regular approach was delivery van taking weekly supplies into the main building. This van if we can call it that had a small engine and struggled to climb the steep drive and it couldn't carry a lot of weight. The biggest weight was the driver himself a portly old guy who was presumed to be just a trader. His family was observed and it appeared that he did not have any other connection with the godfathers than simple trade.

The Fords organised a team of resistance fighters to lie in a circle around the building and the van driver was drugged and removed just before the van came within sight of the villa. Fordy himself ever at the forefront, carefully loaded a wine barrel filled with C4 plastic explosive and detonator, and hid it amongst the loaves and milk. The van was unbelievably slow but its little two stroke engine howled as it successfully negotiated the climb. When it finally stopped Fordy climbed out to find the entrance door to a courtyard that he had just come through still open and an inner door slowly opening. The sleepy man that opened it was instantly aware of a change and demanded to know where the usual driver, Roberto was.

"Oh the old man's got pneumonia, and he really isn't very well" Fordy lied.

The guards suspicions were partly allayed but he demanded that Fordy at least help with the offloading.

Fordy smiled inwardly and grumbling, moved well over half the load onto the courtyard including the large barrel of 'port'.

"Be careful with that!" ordered the guard.

Fordy was very careful for entirely different reasons. The C4 explosive was safe enough under most circumstances but Fordy was not so confident of the hastily made detonator.

Nevertheless he took the tip surprisingly offered by the guard and put the coins in his pocket.

He went to the van and found that the engine would not start probably due to its worn old state and the guard laughed and said "no change there then!" Fordy pushed the van round in a tight circle and the guard helped him push it out side. Once outside the vehicle would roll and Fordy pushed his foot on the clutch and engaged bottom gear. He let the clutch out as the van gathered a little speed and finally the engine spluttered into life. He looked in the mirror and could see the laughing guard waving. He waited a few seconds and tooted the feeble horn. The guard had gone inside and had gone to fetch his little stack truck. He had loaded one pile of goods onto it and had taken these to the larder area when the bomb went off. There was earthquake like damage to the building, it collapsed onto itself and yet one or two people staggered out of the ruins, trying to cough the dust from their lungs. Peter Ford's men were however already emerging from their cover and quickly covered the safety distance they had allowed, entering the courtyard or rather what remained of it. Their silenced weapons coughed three times then once more. They listened and waited for any sign of life. There was none and they retreated and swiftly went their separate ways.

The bang had awakened the whole of the local town and as the morning mist lifted the column of rising dust was still visible. The incident was portrayed in the press as a gangland revenge killing, mostly because only the mob would dare do such a thing. After the reformation when so many over privileged types were unable to reclaim their former wealth, those with mob wealth had been seemingly unaffected. Their ostentatious life style remained and thus their true positions were revealed. No one in the town mourned the loss of those in the villa and there had been a number of hoodlums visiting when the bomb went off. The place was somewhat cleansed.

Both Ford brothers knew that this would not be the end of the matter. The mob had been resilient and would still be resilient they had no doubt. It would though create a period of in fighting as other factions vied with each other for the upper hand. At least the immediate threat to the Space administration had been removed. Peter Ford was quite deductive and his summation of the situation was that the eliminated bunch had been the first to consider infiltrating efforts in Space, and they had unfortunately shown the way.

While Don Ford militarised the environs of the Space centre making access and exit a controlled exercise, Peter busied himself studying what he might do if he was in a mobster's shoes. In this way he hoped to second guess what the next approach would be, then in cahoots with his brother he would try to forestall any such attempt.

James Whistler was pleased with the way the Fords had conducted themselves since he had employed them and considered the money well spent. James was a believer in democracy and he knew that he would have to be careful in case the security guys themselves got too aggressive. He firmly believed that this would never happen with the Ford brothers in charge, but their small enterprise had grown and he decided he would conduct his own further checks into all of the security employees.

The security men allowed to work within the inner perimeter of the Space administration had their employment records and qualifications recorded. The details were all checked out not by mail but by visiting the persons who had signed their letters of recommendation. So far all checked out properly but James also asked Helen to conduct personal interviews on the premise that someone was due promotion and these were necessary background checks.

Helen was delightfully subtle with meaningful questions asked at apparently random moments, so much so that not one person did what Fordy had done and realised that there was a double meaning to some of her questions.

Helen would then study the responses and so far she agreed that there did not appear to be a security threat close at hand.

Meanwhile Judder and Smed were busy trying to perfect a negative matter container.

CHAPTER 21

THE CONTAINER

Working closely together Judder and Smed found a great mutual respect. They discussed the requirements long into the nights over several days. They both knew of diamond and its remarkable strength. They both knew of laboratory experiments using the hexagonal structure of graphite with artificially created bonds. This produced material with what they hoped would be a strong enough material for their purpose. Research starting in the twentieth century produced a substance called 'Lonsdaleite' after the woman who discovered it, by using graphite to start with. In its purest form this was harder than natural diamond by some 58 %.

The Triton diamond shards were similar in structure to Lonsdaleite, and were so hard it was first thought that machining it would be impossible. Where there is a will there is a way and the industrial engineers soon cracked the problems and expanded and rolled the diamond lattice which was in its turn rolled into various metals giving them fantastic strength.

In this case though, means would have to be found to allow machining of the basic crystal.

Judder suggested enlisting the help of the mining engineers on Triton. These men had marvelled at the strange way that the crystals grew and were mightily intrigued by the nature of the crystal growing catalyst which left the diamond soft for some hours before it hardened.

Smed agreed with Judder on this point and considered that the only way to cut the anti matter from FB1 would be to construct a fluted tube that could be screwed into the core of the fireball from somewhere a few feet from its centre. He hoped to be able to cool the middle of the tube and also hoped to rely on the brilliant thermal conductivity of the diamond to stop the cutting edge from melting and blunting.

Judder suggested that a disc be fixed inside the cutting spiral, with a rod that would allow the disc to be raised as soon as cutting was judged finished. This he thought would interfere with the cooling of the tip slightly and thus the diamond cutting edge would melt and amalgamate with the disc forming a natural massively strong gas tight seal. Judder though wondered how it would be possible to seal the other end of the tube. He grinned with shear delight when he heard Smed's proposal. Smed's idea was to ensure that the other end was already sealed. The operating rod and disc would be inside the tube and an electromagnet would be used to push the disc into its sealing position at the appropriate moment. Smed had calculated that the magnetic material was positioned in the coolest part of the tube and should be cool enough to avoid going through its Curie point where it would loose it magnetic qualities.

"That is the difference between sciences and engineering, I suppose!" he smiled again at the simplicity of that idea. Since the acquisition of FB1 matter was to be done coming in from space the tube would already have a vacuum in it and thus there would be no need to allow an escape for trapped air or gasses.

They were ready now to involve the scientists. Science would give the best estimate of the depth required to probe, the likely temperatures and then how to supercool the captured sample.

Smed again saw no problem in cooling the sample. "Just leave it in Space for a few hours in the shade somewhere and it will cool down naturally. The thing then will be to keep it that cool and I think the scientists may tell us what the danger temperature is likely to be!"

"I think we should go on a mini mission to Triton and find out all we can on the growing processes, they are already growing shapes and there is a move afoot to grow a whole jet engine primary compressor blade, so the boys up there know what they are doing!" added Judder.

"We need to speak to James Whistler, Judder!"

CHAPTER 22

THE WHISTLER CONSIDERS THE IDEAS AND SENDS A SMALL MISSION

James Whistler listened carefully to the ideas put before him, and he agreed that the grown diamond tubes should be possible considering the state of mining expertise on Triton.

He made a mental note to send a small mission onto Triton using the Moneybag as the primary transport.

He agreed with the cooling and thought that natural cooling would be best provided the matter anti matter reaction could be interrupted. He thought that there may be no cooling unless the action could be interrupted, otherwise the sample would simply keep going like a micro sun.

James Whistler mused over the properties of diamond, saying "carbon is probably the most interesting element on earth. It can combine with a vast array of other elements but it can also combine with itself to form diamond or graphite. We have also to note that glassy carbon is a high temperature gas tight element and you may find that useful in your research.

Diamond will melt at 4373 degrees Celsius so it can take a fair amount of heat. I suggest that we try a design where the general temperature is only allowed to reach say 3500 degrees and that leaves a fair safety margin."

Smed listened to what he said and then added his latest thought, "If we consider that Sonny is a ball of known diameter, it will be at maximum temperature at its core. If we shoot a projectile at it designed to scoop some material, we would be best served by shooting slightly off centre and thus helping keep the temperature down, we would retrieve our projectile some distance away. We would probably need two ships, one to fire the missile and one to catch it on the exit side."

Judder added "we could make the receiving ship have a bowl which could have liquid nitrogen squirting nozzles on it to promote the initial cooling and if we get that right then, it should only be a matter of time before the two constituent parts begin to form. In free Space with very little gravitational influence from planetary sources the natural gravity properties of the two constituents will force them apart!"

"Yes it all sounds so easy!" chuckled the Whistler, "Smed you had better prepare your self for your first Space flight, the basic training should take about six weeks, so your family will have time to get used to the idea, in the meantime Judder perhaps you could use your contacts to find out who would be the best mining engineer on Triton.

Please continue your discussions because this manoeuvre will be the most important thing ever tried and I urge patience and care. Go to it!

Note from Catherine Whistler. I have to try to put the next part into my own words because it is too technical for me. I trust and believe that your overall understanding will not be impaired. Smed and Judder did achieve their aim and got a tube containing both necessary constituents.

With considerable engineering effort a new shuttle spacecraft was designed having the heavy gravity motor core distributed around the outside. The general shape was two spheres with a small connecting tube. The newly isolated matter was drawn apart by the cooling methods mentioned before. The diamond shard tube was right at the axis of the ship and ran the length of it. The high voltage and high current controls for the antigravity function were split into two and were distributed in a sphere at each end of the ship.

There was complete independence of control and it was possible to expose none or one or both to the attractions of gravity. An unmanned mission was planned where the general details of the run were to be tried out on positive matter only. Now the antimatter and matter each had their own mini gravity control force field surround very similar to the propulsion motor and the plan was to accelerate up to warp 0.99 then use rocket power to cause the ship to enter the rethe. The on board computor would fire up the rocket motors to exit the rethe and provided that the system functioned ok the ship would come back to momma for a thorough investigation.

Well it worked, the ship registered a few minutes in the rethe and exited exactly as predicted. The technical design engineers went over the ship almost molecule by molecule and found nothing wrong so the mission was set to proceed with stage two again unmanned, well almost.

The entry went exactly to plan and then there was silence as there was no ship exiting. So was no news good news?

Perhaps it was because the time element if correct would have brought the ship back to the real world after about a week.

The ship suddenly re-appeared on the radar and was collected and examined.

On board the ship was a young mouse. The Whistler was incandescent with rage. "Some buffoon has risked the entire Space programme for a god dammed mouse!" he roared.

However it was noticed that the mouse was possibly not a pet but a field mouse. The Whistler was somewhat mollified but he was still irritated that the mouse which could have been part of the experiment was a rogue element.

One of the technicians suggested that the mouse may have got on, 'on the other side' as he put it. The Whistler quietened down immediately while his agile mind considered this, then he had a flash of the Solomons.

He gathered the entire crew of the experiment, spacemen and ground crew and backup, and brought a butcher's cleaver that he borrowed from Nancy Wisdom.

He said that a vital part of the experiment was to see what happened when negative matter met positive matter suddenly, and with that he fetched the mouse from its cage and brought the cleaver whistling down. He guided the blade to just miss the mouse and looked up when he heard an intake of breath. One of the young men from the ground crew was now squirming with embarrassment and made his way to the front as the Whistler beckoned him. "Ok experiment concluded!" some who had not had a clear view of the happening thought the Whistler was crazy to assemble that many folk only to tell them it was all over in only a few seconds.

"I didn't realise I had lost him until the experiment was already under weigh!" wailed the unfortunate.

"James Whistler poured scorn on the young man. "You would have jeopardised an entire spaceship and crew because you did not have the courage to tell anyone of your loss?" he sneered.

The young man looked miserable and crestfallen. "I had three, sir but our family cat had caught and eaten the others, when he knocked the cage over and broke it. As I was late for work already, I rescued him and put him in my breast pocket and took him to work with me. We were all so busy I forgot about him until I got home and then I found I had lost him. I searched the car, and couldn't find him and I had concluded I had lost him at work but it never occurred to me he had got on board the ship. I am truly sorry!"

James Whistler grinned saying "consider yourself a bucket of dog meat that has just been chewed up! I now have a job for you because your mouse is the first living creature to have got into the fourth dimension and come out alive. I want chapter and verse of his life from what you can remember and his future life must be recorded in minute detail. Fail in this duty and you are out! Understood?"

"Yes sir but there is something already sir!"

"Well?"

"This mouse though still quite young was the oldest of the three I had but he had just developed a lump on his one back leg and the lump has gone!"

"Get him examined by a vet and bring the report to me pronto!"

The vet's report gave an absolute clean bill of health to the mouse. The Whistler viewed the animal on a weekly basis. The general reports from the young ground crew member never had anything to say but each week there was a revised report from the vet. This had no abnormalities to report. The young man had the temerity to introduce a white female to the cage and in a very short time a litter of blind mice was born. These grew normally, and so a mollified James Whistler allowed the young man back to normal duties but insisted that the mouse or mice remained effectively in quarantine.

Almost grudgingly the Whistler realised that the young crewmember did have something about him and his mind went back to the days when he too had done something in secret. He smiled inwardly and allowed his mind to consider a manned mission.

In his thoughts the Whistler considered a manned mission of a short nature, to go precisely as the last unmanned mission except the mouse would be replaced by a man. He knew that an experienced man would be required and he knew that new family ties virtually precluded his top men. He decided that he would use the company news sheet to ask for volunteers. The sheet was pinned to various notice boards throughout the halls of the company and he already knew there was one man that would be an ideal candidate. This man knocked on James Whistler's door within half an hour of the news sheet being on the notice board.

"Come in Heinrich!" smiled the Whistler.

"I want to be mission leader!" said Heinrich with typical Germanic coolness and directness.

"You will be considered, along with everyone else!"

"Perhaps you will get a number of volunteers, but I openly threatened to punch three very good men straight in the gob!" grinned Heinrich. He spoke English so well now that his vocabulary included a superb collection of swearwords and vulgar phrases. "I have an ulterior motive as well as my wish to be first. I have been on the cusp of several discoveries and I am the most experienced away team leader. Therefore there is no one better qualified, and I still have no family!" he smiled as James Whistler was effectively cornered by his logic.

"I openly admit that you were my choice before I asked for volunteers and because you have no wife or children. Somehow though, I don't think you have revealed your ulterior motive!"

"Correct! My ulterior motive is based upon a rumour and that is that the mouse had cancer before it went and didn't have it when it got back. Is that true?"

James Whistler raised both eyebrows and looked down at the pencil that he was fiddling with. "Heinrich, I take it that you think you may have this disease. The mouse had a lump and the lump has now gone and it continues to remain healthy. Unfortunately, the mouse was an accidental passenger and I simply do not know what the basis of its lump was."

"I do have a problem and my specialist thinks it is an early sign of cancer, and if I can volunteer the journey will possibly cure me. I have thought about this over the last two hours and you could include my detailed medical record as part of the mission" Heinrich volunteered.

"Ok, I take it that it is still private, this knowledge of your disease. I suggest that you go back to the canteen now and throw a tantrum. Moaning how you, the best man in the Space service, has been turned down by that nerd the Whistler! This should be good for security. In the meantime I will continue to vet other applicants for the next mission. The shuttle ship of the latest design is called the 'Backwards Venture' and she is ready to go immediately. Reaching into his desk he gave Heinrich the ships log. Inside the log was the design features of the ship and Heinrich stared at the first page as he read avidly. He was unaware of the Whistler's comments over the next two or three minutes and waved imperious dismissive fingers in the air as the Whistler tried to dismiss him.

James Whistler fetched two cups of coffee. Heinrich Schmidt unconsciously reached for his coffee and took a sip. It was hot, and he came out of his reverie muttering "Did you say something?"

"Heinrich, I have known you for a while, but I have never known you go so deep so quickly before. Learn that entire design brief and if you want further detail ask Judder or Smed. Here is Smed's card; I don't think you have met him yet have you?"

"I had heard about him and he was at the last party at the Prof's but somehow we never got to have a little natter properly but I noticed him in that office a couple of doors down from Mrs. Svensson's.

With that Heinrich swigged the remains of his coffee, expertly lobbing the cup into the waste bin and shot out of his chair and was gone.

James Whistler was not a man of prayer, but he was close to it as he fervently wished that Heinrich's wish would come true.

Smed found himself staring at this smiling man who he somehow recognised and was just about to ask him who the hell he was when "Heinrich Schmidt!" was spoken.

"Of course, from the party. Hello Heinrich! I didn't recognise you in uniform so to speak." A short while later Smed was taken with the man who asked very pertinent questions about the controls of the ship. The manual prepared had all of the answers and he pointed Heinrich to each paragraph as the questions came thick and fast.

Finally Heinrich stood and clicked his heels in salute. "Ah you are German," said Smed "best of luck in whatever you are doing!"

Heinrich studied as if it was the last thing he would ever do, and he privately wondered whether this would be the case.

He considered that the matter anti matter issue was the cleverest thing about the latest ship and he knew that he would have to jettison the antimatter if the temperature system came to develop a fault. He decided that if at all possible he would jettison it in the real world and trust that the resulting reaction when it sought and found its companion amount of positive matter would be a mini- Sonny and not a cataclysmic bang. He studied that part of the manual intensely and realised that he would have to jettison the whole diamond shard tube and so the matter and anti matter would be a balanced amount so it may even cool off again in open Space and would be re-harvestable. He asked Smed about this point and Smed agreed. So Heinrich acquired a marker buoy of the type used in early asteroid harvesting. He would use this as a marker. He decided that he would be fully suited at all times and would fit his helmet the moments before he would enter the rethe. He also decided he would verbally record his every thought, and start video's at perceived moments of interest or danger.

The day of the mission was upon him while his newly acquired knowledge was fresh in his mind and he found his ship approaching warp 0.98 when he fitted his helmet and closed the visor. He watched as the ship automatically gave a blast on the rocket motors and felt the shudder as he went into the rethe. Even inside his space suit he could hear the whistle from the magnetic and electrostatic control system as the real matter shield closed down and the anti matter shield opened up. The characteristic hum was slightly different. His heart rate was high so he thought and spoke his fear for the voice recorder. Suddenly the rocket motors blasted again and he was through to the other side. The shudder was still there but different in its feel and then the glass smoothness of normal Space travel resumed. He looked out of the window speaking his thoughts and was aware of a dull ache in his back.

The normal black velvet background peppered with silver spots was replaced by deep blue velvet spattered with red spots he almost held his breath and suddenly found the emotion of jealousy flood his mind as he thought of the mouse. Ludicrous. Absolutely ludicrous. There was an electronic clock on board and it wasn't exactly going backwards but it kept fading then every so often the digits would illuminate and the number displayed was definitely going down! He had had the foresight to bring an old fashioned mechanical wristwatch, inherited from his father and when he looked this watch was still going but normally. 'It cannot go backwards' he thought 'its design simply doesn't allow that'. He suddenly worried that he and the ship were intruders. They were after all positive matter and were scooting along in an anti matter world. He looked at the mission clock. This was still operating normally and one hour later he felt the ship change course slightly as it sought what he hoped would be a blue portal. The rocket motors blasted and nothing at all happened as a result but a second blast produced a reaction in the ship and the third blast produced a high frequency shriek as the ship escaped the anticlockwise world and got back into what he fervently hoped was the rethe. Again he heard the characteristic whine of the electronic controls as the negative matter was shielded and the positive matter was exposed. This was the status quo for about five minutes until the rocket motors blasted again. The usual shudder this time and then lo and behold the Solar system came into view.

He opened radio contact and calmly gave out the agreed call sign. "Backward Venture is forward!"

The rest of this small step for mankind went without a hitch of any sort.

Heinrich refused to go through a debriefing session until he had seen his surgeon.

"Heinrich the best news that I can give to most of my patients is that the disease is in remission. Your problem has gone to such a degree that I wonder whether or not I looked at the wrong scans and x-rays before. You are I am pleased to say completely healthy!

After exiting the surgery Heinrich insisted on a private head to head with the Whistler before going to be debriefed.

"James it would appear that I am cured. But not only that I feel a freedom in my mind that is almost inexplicable. It is as though some form of disorder has been replaced with calm order!"

"James Whistler had a moment of inspiration and gave Heinrich a cryptic crossword puzzle to do. Now it was known that Heinrich loved these puzzles and five minutes later he commented, "Ok James I've done that but why did you ask me to do it?"

"Heinrich unless I am much mistaken you have just beaten your best ever time!"

Heinrich glanced at his watch, grinned "Christ I have, not by much, but I'm sure you are right!"

"Debriefing for you now Heinrich, miss nothing out. However our two little more recent discoveries are best kept quiet for the moment."

"I was aware that I had a dull ache in my back just after I exited the rethe on the other side, but I was so struck by the different view that I had no time to dwell on it so I didn't notice when it disappeared. If push comes to shove though I would say whatever went on it was during the transition from clockwise to anti clockwise worlds. The only other thing is that I think captain Johnson and the Prof were actually the first humans to have gone through the rethe and out the other side!"

"What on earth makes you say that?"

"Well the Prof clearly described seeing the deep blue velvet spotted with red pinpricks of light, and when actually in the rethe it is utterly black. The other view does not come into being until you are actually through to the negative time space continuum!"

"He will be intrigued when I tell him that, because it implies that you can penetrate without all of the fuss we have tried!"

CHAPTER 23

THE DEBRIEFING

Heinrich expected a myriad of carefully controlled questions but what he actually got was a plethora of excited schoolboy enquiries asking what it was like.

Heinrich suddenly found himself in charge of his own debriefing.

"Gentlemen, be professional!" Heinrich waited for the hubbub to die down. "I will admit that my pulse rate went through the roof as one cannot escape the idea of sudden oblivion, and that is an unpleasant moment. I had already enclosed myself in my Space suit and closed my visor before the jump into the rethe. With the new design of ship there is a dual anti gravity mark 2 motor. The positive matter one, the normal one, covers the outside of the rear half of the ship, which is where I resided. Now this appears to function exactly like the normal mark 2 motor in spite of the fact that it is a shell rather than a core. Because you find yourself sitting inside the shell the electrostatic and electromagnetic drives make a characteristic noise, and this is plainly audible. After jumping into the rethe, I heard the hum of the control slowly diminish as the normal control is switched to full cover. You will have to ask the engineers why this is so. A short while later the anti matter one began its slightly different hum as it exposed itself. Now the controls for the hull antigravity shells are duplicated with miniature ones for each chunk of matter so the small amount of anti matter is exposed just as the small amount of matter is hidden. The main hull forward shell control also opens at the same time so that the rethe can detect the anti matter quantity which will be in the ascendency as there is a clever second function of the smaller antigravity functions. The real or positive matter is almost entirely cloaked, as the negative matter is simultaneously exposed. Ok so far there was nothing frightening, but then the ships computor fired the rockets and you get the juddering sensation except that the feel of it is different. A bit like two musical instruments tuned to the same note for example a violin and a saxophone. The sound is the same yet different then I was through and the vibrationless glass smooth feel of normal Space travel resumed.

I freely admit that my mind was stunned for several seconds, but as I took stock of what was happening I looked out of the viewing window.

There instead of black velvet with silver pinpricks, I saw dark blue velvet covered in red pinpricks.

The so called questioners were spellbound. Heinrich continued, "I looked at the digital clock on my control console and the digits kept fading and flashing. Each time they flashed on the number displayed was definitely reducing. From that I concluded rightly or wrongly that I was going backward in time. I also took as my personal memento a wristwatch inherited from my late father, and when I looked at this it was still going but still going forward. I concluded that a watch such as that simply cannot go backwards the mechanical mechanism precludes the possibility. I took my own pulse rate at this juncture and this was still going at about 150 or so. Well I was still excited and somewhat fearful!

Bear in mind that this mission was not manned in the normal sense of the word. I was on board to simulate the effect of a mouse!"

There were a few chuckles from the audience as most of them knew how a mouse had effectively evaded all of the security measures on the previous mission.

"After what seemed an eternity but in essence only a few minutes I felt the ship change course as it was programmed to do and then I prayed fervently that it would find a blue portal so I could come home. When it fired up the rockets with a 10 second blast, it produced no jump. It fired another blast of about 15 seconds and this produced a reaction. When I looked out of the viewing window I saw a funnel like distortion to my view, before I could photograph this, the rockets fired a third time and then I felt the similar shudder to the entry shudder, but it was accompanied by a deathly sort of shriek. Then I was back into the rethe. The characteristic whine of the ships controls were audible as the ship hid the anti matter and then exposed the positive matter. Another blast on the rockets and I was back in the Solar system.

No doubt you will study all of the data retrievable, and if I may suggest that you disperse and do this, then question me again and I will respond. I consider that this debriefing is over. Good morning gentlemen!"

With that Heinrich stood and walked to the coffee machine and helped himself.

James Whistler, Judder and Smed sat at the back making notes. James Whistler wrote furiously as he watched Heinrich. This was the first time that any one had handled his own debriefing and James marvelled at the easy way in which Heinrich handled it all. He brought to mind the comment Heinrich had made to him about how his mind had suddenly become clearer, and at the moment he was the only person other than Heinrich to know of this.

If Heinrich stayed clear of cancer, then he could see there would be a whole host of requests for trips to the other side from the medical profession, as soon as the results were made public. The Whistler also knew that the little mouse was still in robust health and seemed more curious and cute than most mice. The Whistler didn't think that the trip had improved the basic intelligence of a mouse but it did seem to have maximised it, and he was sure the same thing had happened to Heinrich Schmidt. Somehow the journey had re-established the curiosity of youth when all living things were at their best, and Heinrich suddenly found himself raised in the pecking order for such things as snooker and darts.

He wasn't unbeatable but he seemed to have improved power of concentration. Heinrich was and is a strong minded individual, and had come through his experience basically improved. The Whistler felt that a weak minded person may not so easily be able to handle the shock to the system.

Later that day he confided in Helen, she thought exactly what Heinrich had suggested, namely that all of the data be studied and then go far a second debriefing. The Whistler had already decided he would do this and asked his senior Space captains and the Prof over for this purpose.

In the event the debriefing scientists had questions that were legion. Heinrich answered most of them, though even with his better ordered mind some were simply outside his knowledge.

One young man sitting at the back asked some very well reasoned questions and the Whistler knew instinctively that this man had a secondary agenda; finally he asked Heinrich simply if he was cured of cancer.

Heinrich never even flinched under the directness of the question but exclaimed "Cancer! What on earth are you asking me that for?"

The young man, who must have had inside knowledge exclaimed, "well it cured the mouse, and what I want to know is has it cured you?"

"What mouse was that!" grinned Heinrich, "surely you don't want me to admit that I was jealous of a mouse and invented a story just so I could guarantee being the first man into the fourth dimension. What a puerile thought!"

The Whistler knew that security had been breached and that the young man was almost certain to be a reporter.

The reporter was not yet satisfied. "You are known to have visited a surgeon before and after your flight!" he persisted.

"I am afraid he did that at my insistence!" chimed in the Whistler, "and pray what do you know of the mouse!"

The reporter looked directly at James Whistler and knew his cover was blown. He was encouraged though as no one wanted to call security.

"I heard from a pet shop about some mice purchased by one of your operatives, and the pet shop owner was sure that one mouse had a problem with his one back leg when he sold it! I believe that the mouse is actually fully recovered now!"

"Your knowledge on the personal history of an ordinary mouse far exceeds that of our personnel department!" the Whistler smiled and decided to come virtually clean about the incident. "I am the Whistler. I dare say my name has figured in your newspaper from time to time. The mouse did have an infection in its leg but it didn't stop it from evading our full security and getting aboard an unmanned mission. I admit that the mouse doesn't have the infection now but all infections of that nature heal quickly under zero gravity conditions. Some of our larger missions have taken many animals as part of a farming function to feed the mission personnel. As a matter of fact your suggestion of healing powers is an interesting one and we will redouble our efforts in recording such matters just to see if there is a wonderful healing quality, but don't hold your breath. After the debriefing is over I invite you to my office and you can enlighten me further. Thank you!" he returned to his apparent day dream state but his mind was running at massive speed as he did not want this piece of healing information to become public knowledge, not yet anyway.

Finally Heinrich began to tire under the constant barrage of questions, and the Whistler decided that the questions were going over old ground so he called a halt to proceedings. As the debriefers filed out he signalled to the reporter and to Heinrich to follow him. Both men followed the few yards to the Whistler's office. James Whistler locked the office door. Seeing a small sign of alarm on the reporters face smoothly said "Just to keep intruders out, I assure you!"

Heinrich instinctively realising that his cancer cure should remain a closely guarded secret spoke first. "Well young man, what's all this about cancer then?"

"So its true then" gasped the reporter "I only jumped to that conclusion because of the mouse and the fact that you visited the surgeon's office at both ends of your trip!"

The Whistler chuckled "I wish some of the wallahs round here were as perceptive as you, but in fact you are just wrong. It would be lovely if you were right, but life simply isn't like that: you can write your story about the mouse if you like because we are simply not in a position to confirm or deny that, as the mouse was a pet and shouldn't have been on the site. We don't want animal rights nutters besieging our doors so you must decide yourself what you wish to write.

Thinking of that I suppose if you had been correct about the cancer cure in humans we would be besieged for an entirely different reason.

By the way Heinrich you are not ill in that way are you? because if you are my life will be hell. You know what the religious nutters are like. They already think we are interfering in god's work and as such we are completely evil."

"Well are you interfering with it?"

"I suppose if you were to poll the crews of the mission ships you might find someone who believed that. The crews are chosen from a deliberate mix of every religion on the planet plus a good smattering of those who are agnostic or atheists. They have been in Space when we harvested some water carrying asteroids and then an atomic bomb one which became Sonny; you know the secondary sun that is helping life on mars. We have had a hand in all this but the creation of all of the component parts is simply down to god. We tried to do the same thing as Sonny elsewhere but we failed miserably, as god or lady luck or whatever you want to call it was not with us.

If we find that there is a possibility of curing cancer then we would make sure that you would be amongst the first to know. It is an intriguing concept. There have been massive advances in our understanding of Space travel and the like and perhaps we have got a little in front of ourselves. I am a cautious man and I don't like and will never send a man on a mission where there is massive risk to the crew. Heinrich here will vouch for that. I suppose some of the Space crew think I am an old woman worrying over nothing. I insist however on having absolutely as many answers as possible before embarking on any venture.

Heinrich chipped in "I think the crews have a little more respect than that for you Mr. Whistler. I myself was on a mission to one of the moons of Saturn and we discovered long amino acid strings there; now these are the essential building blocks of life. The place was so cold that life couldn't possibly evolve. But we took some of these on board our ship and before you knew it we had an epidemic on board. We managed to recover from that being isolated out in Space, but imagine what would have happened if the disease had had a longer incubation period. We could have brought it back to earth and we would have had a plague of biblical proportions. Fortunately all samples were gathered together and ejected into Space.

Mr. Whistler has expressed the view that we should never visit that place again, and I must say I agree. The space service has away teams to explore such places and I am the most senior of the participants. It is quite a responsible job, and I have just had a mental image of going through a sort of cleansing station to get rid of any diseases, but I don't suppose it will ever be like that. We do go through hose downs and the water used is ejected into Space so as to avoid cross contamination and the Space suits spend an hour in a nuclear radiated part of the ships. But really that is it. So far I have remained in good health." He tapped the wooden table with his fingers.

"What newspaper do you work for?" asked James Whistler.

"I work for a private small time publisher that occasionally gets things published in the Reader's Digest, and other responsible publications! And I must say I have always regarded myself as a non sensational author except if there is something sensational to report. I am Adam Round."

"Ok Mr. Round I don't think that we can tell you anything else but an idea has occurred to me. My second in command here in headquarters has the responsibility of keeping the outside world informed of our activities, and I am sure she would dearly love to divest herself of that activity. It can be an onerous task because each ship that we send out has about 18000 or so folk on board. It would cause untold family trauma if the wrong details were precipitously leaked out. Now she has carried out this role with distinction. Perhaps you would like such a role for yourself!"

"You are offering me a job?" squeaked Adam Round.

"Not exactly, with your present position you may consider that a means to shut you up. But I think you could make a contribution here so write your story completely unfettered by us and then give us a bell. James handed over his card and Adam Round nodded in acknowledgment and put it into his wallet. He stood to leave and nodded at the door. James Whistler grinned and entered the unlock code. He watched the departing figure and picked up the phone and dialled Fordy.

"We have just interviewed a certain Adam Round!" and he then outlined the general goings on and Fordy said "is he of slight build about medium height? If he is, he is just leaving the building!" the Whistler gleaned a single frame from his office security camera and transmitted it to Fordy.

"Security checks on him and find out how he got in here please!"

CHAPTER 24

SECURITY CHECKS ON ADAM ROUND

Fordy's checks revealed no mob connections. Both he and Peter Ford were glad of that. If Adam Round could get in so easily then so could the mob. Peter Ford examined the security records and could find no breach but both of the Ford brothers knew there had to be a simple explanation. Peter Ford wondered whether or not Adam round was a twin because many of the DNA based security checks could be sidestepped by the likeness. A few days later making no progress they were in the canteen when Peter suddenly did a double take.

There sitting facing them as large as life was Adam Round. Fordy got up and went round the table intent on having a quiet word, but opposite him was another Adam Round. Turning the situation to his advantage spoke easily to the brothers. "Well I thought me and my brother here were the only twins working at the Space admin.!"

The reply was "Yes you could still be that!"

"Triplets?" Peter enquired.

"Quads! But our sister died in infancy. We are fully natural quads no egg fertilisation for our dad!"

"Where is your brother?" asked Fordy in his most genial way.

"Oh he doesn't work here; he is a reporter for some little down town rag!"

Fordy decided to come clean "hello I'm Don and this is Peter, we are joint heads of the 'New Security Company' that keeps rogues out."

"Ok, ok I lost my security badge about a month ago, but I reported it and had a new one issued. Surely I haven't transgressed?"

"No I don't think either of you have!" said Peter.

"Adam!" said the other two, "but how the hell did he get round the finger print test?"

A couple of hours later Peter Ford turned up at Adam's apartment but he was out. Two hours later he returned and Peter Ford walked swiftly to catch him up. "Afternoon Adam!" he said cheerily, making no attempt to hide his Space centre jacket.

Adam knew he had been rumbled and invited Peter in.

After introductions, Adam admitted that security at the Space centre was tight and said he had had a devils game to get in.

"About a month ago I was coming out of my brothers flat when I noticed a credit card lying in the road. I picked it up and realised that actually it was a Space Centre security badge so I kept it. Reporter's nose you know! Well from what my brothers had said I knew I would have a game with finger prints but I managed to lift a set from a wine glass and I had them printed on a clear sticky sheet. Then I cut them out and stuck them to latex gloves.

As I went to the security machine I suddenly couldn't remember which was left and which was right but my guess was bang on and I was in!

I had listened to the scuttlebutt from my brothers and made a few deductions of my own and then I was into the debriefing lecture. I asked questions and on about my fourth question, Mr. Whistler twigged that I was an outsider, but he let me go on then basically offered me a job. I still haven't decided whether or not to accept it; and now you know everything!"

"Peter Ford smiled and said "well not only did you get in, you baffled us security experts as well. I think you must be congratulated. I must admit that we will now go for something that has been under consideration for a while and you wouldn't have got round it so easily, we are trialling a palm print recogniser that also detects sweat!"

"No subtle threats about my publishing then?"

"We are charged with security for the Space administration we are not a political party trying to eliminate free speech. I have no instructions that tell me that there is an emergency situation developing, but I do hope you will consider the offer you have. I would rather work alongside you than against you!" Peter Ford then took his leave.

Adam Round knew that the Space administration had taken the breach of their security seriously but had not over-reacted; all in all he thought so long as my article doesn't offend them I feel disposed towards taking up the job offer.

His article when published contained no direct claims about healing the sick or even raising the dead; but it subtly left doors open so that a follow up article could be knitted seamlessly in and cover these very points.

James Whistler read the article and found himself admiring the way that the reporter had not given up on his original ideas but had cleverly left doors ajar a fraction. He hoped that he would hear from Adam Round again.

There were no more repercussions from the last mission and after almost two months his PA told him there was an Adam Round waiting downstairs in reception. James went down in the lift.

"Ah Mr. Round I had given up hope of hearing from you. I read your article and I was very impressed with it!"

"Thank you Mr. Whistler, I just wish my editor shared your view! Perhaps we could discuss your recent offer?"

James issued him a day pass and took him up to his office.

"Perhaps you were a bit too subtle for your editor but I could see how skilfully you had worded the article ready for a bit of future stretch. Should you take up the offer that I will make to you, you will need every ounce of your perception and skill to handle the information that comes your way. For example, the Space teams discovered diamond shards on Triton, one of the moons of Neptune. We needed time to get all of our backers to the Space centre so that we could inform them of our discovery simultaneously, any other method would have been seen as favouring one or more against some of the others. We needed a fortnight to do the job and in the end we did manage to keep a lid on things for three weeks, but there was one perceptive reporter who almost broke our security shroud, and it took a clever bit of shifting to convince him of our little fib!"

"I remember that he accused the Prof of having a diamond walking stick but it turned out to be just a fancy piece of araldite!"

"Sure thing but the one the Prof was really trying out was real diamond. We weren't sure of the diamond find and the Prof used one as a walking stick as part of our efforts."

Just to hark back to your cancer cure idea. Imagine for a minute that you are correct. There was a point in history in the early twentieth century where a scientist realising that rogue cell multiplication was the reason that death ensued in a cancer patient. He found how to stop cell replenishment and gave an operation to one or two patients; the result was a success in the short term, but their bodies became ancient very quickly and the results were so horrendous that the operation was banned for ever."

"So imagining that my guess was a bull's eye then it would have been irresponsible to have revealed results too early!"

"Perhaps in the eye of a young reporter no, but in my eyes yes."

"If I accept your offer it would place me at the other side of the picture immediately!"

"Perhaps yes perhaps no. You would be privy to a host of sensitive information and you would soon see that rushing into publicise things too early can often ruin the advantage presented when a discovery is made. I realise that you may prefer the maverick existence but I truly hope you will not. I have already drafted out a basic contract of employment for you to consider. It would be a well paid job. Here in Space administration we cannot proceed on the basis of suspicion, we go for straight fact. The security boys are the only ones who would operate on that sort of basis and you would have direct contact with them to voice suspicions that are below our radar for example, but primarily you would offer statements to the press, concerning our efforts in Space and we would rely on you to keep the wolves from baying at our doors. Before any offer is made final, you would have to undergo a full security check. You have already been partly investigated and you have two siblings here so I don't expect any skeletons in cupboards. Unless you have some confession that you would like to declare now?"

Adam Round considered this and said "well I haven't always been an angel but I haven't got any wild political aspirations or agenda, so perhaps you could give me your offer and find me a corner to sit in while I look at it?"

Here is your offer, the canteen is two floors down come and see me before the end of the day even if you are still studying. He picked up the internal phone "Nancy, James here I have a young man by the name of Adam Round. He is coming down to study a file and I imagine he will get hungry so give him complimentary meals. How is Jarvis? Ah oh really, he moves almost as fast as me!"

Adam Round went to the canteen and Nancy Wisdom gave him a full dinner and sat him down in a quiet corner well away from the kitchen end. "How many more of you are there?" she enquired.

"I am the last one!" he grinned. He recognised a good general feel to the place and suddenly found that he simply trusted James Whistler. Although he was the head honcho, there was no side on the man. He did not converse in corporation speak. Adam grinned to himself. He still felt sure that there was a link to cancer cure, but half of his soul simply wanted to know, the other half wanted to publish, but he knew he could come to terms with that. The salary offered was generous as were holidays. He had a girl and they had been wondering how they could possibly consider ordinary things like house home and family. It would all be possible with this offer. He knew with such a generous offer his life wouldn't be entirely his own but he was not selling his soul. His brothers had always spoken of the Space centre with a small reverence and he suddenly knew they were right. He suffered an internal capitulation; he was suddenly a company man. Only a few days ago he would have recoiled with horror at the thought, but now he looked forward to a very different work life.

He sat back and smiled as he could see Nancy Wisdom bringing him a cup of tea.

"I know your brothers prefer tea so I hope you like it as well!" she smiled.

My brothers are also chocolate biscuit mad!" he grinned and was then acknowledging that she was ahead of the game as she reached inside her pinafore tabard thing and produced a whole packet. "You will all be as fat as pigs!" she chided as she walked away.

Adam Round reflected for a moment on the death of his sister before he was even old enough to remember her she had been Eve and his brothers were Cain and Abel. They had been born in that order and had been so named by a cheery midwife. Their parents had been unable to think of better names so the die had been set. He ate a few biscuits put the rest into his briefcase and went in search of the Whistler. He was just coming out of his office in something of a rush when Adam said "I accept!"

"Right ho we will be in touch!" shouted the Whistler as he rushed along the corridor.

That night as Adam sat in his flat with his girlfriend they looked out onto a grey scene. It was not yet dark but the rain lashed down with a vengeance. The wind howled and caused the kitchen ventilator to rattle. "There goes our former life out of here double quick!" he joked, but inside he still feared that something would go wrong. He had wrestled with his conscience when he offered his article to his editor and he had known that it simply was not colourful enough. There wasn't anything about vice or corruption or any of the baser things in life that he could easily have dredged up from his fertile mind. Even then he knew his future was likely to be tied up with the Space centre and didn't want to do anything to put that in jeopardy.

After a few days the offer was made final there had been no security issues. He sent an e-mail straight back saying he was delighted to accept and he would be available from about five weeks time as he had to work at least a calendar month's notice.

CHAPTER 25

ADAM'S LIFE CHANGES VERY QUICKLY

When he breezed into work the next morning his editor already had a number of tasks to do. Adam without ado handed his editor an envelope and told him of his desire to work elsewhere.

"Where at?" said the editor through gritted teeth.

"The Space centre!" said Adam.

"Oh, right, they bought you off then I've a good mind to phone in and tell them of some of the tricks you've pulled to get stories!" he sneered and picked up the phone. Adam watched and without a flicker of emotion mentioned a certain building that the editor visited frequently. The editor put the phone down.

"You cannot imagine that you have been going there for the best part of ten years without someone here knowing about it. Christ we are all newshounds!" he paused.

"Will a months notice be ok?"

"A months notice? You won't be getting any more pay I can tell you that, so as far as I am concerned you can pick up your pay and get the hell out of my newspaper!" Adam went to the office and told the lady in there that he was leaving effective immediately.

While he was emptying his desk the editor realising he had been hasty tried to make amends, but Adam would have none of it.

"It wasn't me that found out about your predilection for fat older women you know. I must be about the fourth to know. You have effectively sacked me so I am going. Don't worry I shall not be taking you to a tribunal; I won't have the time or inclination. And with regard to the Space centre buying me off you could be right. The price I asked for and got was decency. Something that hasn't been seen around here for some time!" and with that he calmly went down to his car to put his belongings in and then went back to the office to collect his dues. The lady in there was a quiet lady and she said. "I am sorry to see you go Mr. Adam. You have been like breath of fresh air round here. I shall miss you". Adam leant across and gave her a peck on the cheek and said "you deserve better than this Mary, I don't know how you have put up with it all these years!" With that he was gone, she thought "go for it lad!" and smiled through her tears.

The following day he recounted the events to the Whistler and apologised for turning up five weeks earlier than he had planned. James Whistler pulled the necessary strings to get full and proper identification and security cards issued and then said. "Adam we are short of personnel around here at the moment. Quite frequently you will be away from your desk attending press conferences; you will need a secretary if not a full blown PA."

"Mr. Whistler, if you will permit I know an ideal person for such a job. She is a lady of mature years and is intensely loyal. She has known me for some years and is used to my personal traits. Could I possibly offer her a position with say equal pay to her present position?"

"No you can't. What you can do is take me to her or her to me and I will interview her myself," commanded the Whistler.

"Please bear with me" asked Adam, he dialled and a very tearful Mary answered the phone. "Hello Mary, its me Adam what are you crying for?"

Mary sobbed and drew sudden breath. "Mr. Adam when the editor found out that I made up your pay to include your portion of holiday pay he almost punched me. I have never seen him so angry, any way he didn't but he has sacked me. Me who's has been here almost twenty five years, what am I going to do?"

Adam had not yet got the hang of the phone system and had had it on loud speaker.

"Tell her you have a job offer for her and you will bring a man round to see her tonight! said the Whistler grimly.

"Mary I am in an office at the moment and my new boss is in here with me. He wants me to bring him around to yours tonight. But I don't know where you live! Don't forget to put your own wages up to include your holiday pay. We will see you at seven tonight" he scribbled furiously as she gave him her address.

Later that evening as Adam Round introduced James Whistler, Mary stood in awe. "Are you really the Whistler? She sniffed; I have read those books by your daughter you know!"

"She is actually my grand daughter-in-law" he smiled.

"Huh, the Whistler in my house!" she perked up and shot off into the kitchen. She had a tray with three cups and a full teapot and milk jug when she returned.

"Thank you Mary, Adam has told me of you on the drive over here."

"Mr. Whistler, Adam was like breath of fresh air in that office. The editor has leaned on every person to occupy that desk and only Adam seemed to have the mentality to resist him. Slowly they all wilted and became like him, completely cynical, and that was such a shame. I must admit I didn't expect to get the sack not for doing my job right anyhow!"

"Adam here will have need of a secretary. This will mean answering and forwarding e-mails or phone calls, and keeping his appointment register; and occasionally making a good cup of tea. Do you think you can handle it?"

"I certainly can and I can do shorthand. There can't be many of us left can there who can do that?"

James Whistler was quietly impressed with this unassuming lady. He scribbled on a piece of paper taken from his wallet and handed it to her. She read it smiled and said "right! Take me to a cheap hotel because he will be round trying to offer me my job back and I don't want it!"

James Whistler said "have you got one of these yet?" and he showed his company credit card to Adam. Adam had but he realised guiltily that he hadn't signed it. Mary was ensconced in a medium class hotel for the night and she was delighted when none other than James Whistler turned up to collect her the following morning.

"I will admit to a certain misgiving yesterday when young Adam turned up for work and asked me if he could offer you a job. He hadn't even been an active employee when he made that request, but I thought you may be worth a look.

Now I hope you like what you see because much hinges on it." They arrived at the Space centre and James escorted Mary, Mary Mustow as it happened and provided her with a daily pass. She was taken up to the top but one floor and ushered into Adam Round's office. James Whistler showed her the rudiments of the telephone system when the phone rang. Mary looked nervously across at him and she picked up the phone and selected the line with the flashing light. "Good morning, Adam Round's office. How can I help you?"

"This is Don Ford here I am trying to track James Whistler down!"

"Just one minute Mr. Ford I will see if I can help. She put her hand over the mouthpiece and said there is a Mr. Don Ford on trying to track you down, are you in?"

"I am, buzz it across to the office phone I think that is the right hand button. She looked at the console grunted and pressed the left hand button. The office phone rang. The Whistler picked the phone up, "morning Fordy I have another task for you on the security front, I would like you to check out a Mrs. Mary Mustow."

"Ok who is she?" asked Fordy.

"She is the lady who just answered the phone" said the Whistler.

"You're not playing away already are you?"

"No, absolutely not, it is just that this lady suddenly found herself out of work and one of our new guys is in need of a secretary so I struck while the iron was hot, so to speak!" the Whistler grinned at the shear cheek of the question.

"Mary, you are a temporary employee at the moment your rate of pay will be advised to you in about ten minutes just sit there and answer the phone. Ring me if anything crops up that you can't handle. Follow the signs down to the canteen. Lunch is three parts of an hour, starting at 13.00 hrs. Ask for Nancy Wisdom and tell her I sent you or she may not let you have a meal!"

"Lunch break, oooh this is a really posh place!" joked Mary.

The Whistler did like what he saw and he watched on the office video link as she explored the desk and took out a list and taped it to the sliding board in her desk. She looked at the phone console and buzzed the various buttons to check on response and then Adam Round came in. "Morning Mary" he said as if he had been saying it for years, which actually he had.

"Coffee would be nice!" he said. She looked at her watch and said "you will have to wait until lunch time I'm afraid!" but she got up grinning and said "it's a pity this machine doesn't work I shall have to go exploring for it!"

"Try inserting this" he said as he gave her a strange looking fob. Within seconds she had inserted it in the machine and two coffees were served up.

She said "I do not know how you pulled this off but I cannot express my gratitude greatly enough." A knock on the door and an imposing man strode in.

"Just thought I'd introduce myself I'm—

"Captain Johnson" finished Mary, mouth half agape.

"Ah yes hello Mary" said Captain Johnson "I've heard of you!"

"But you can't have" gasped Mary "I haven't even been employed yet!"

"As a secretary you will be expected to keep tabs on all the scuttlebutt that comes your way, and I think maybe you should read this!" he handed her a small folder. She began to read and a slow smile crossed her features particularly when she read the salary. She finished and asked Captain Johnson if he would thank James Whistler in person for her. Just at that moment Helen Svensson came in and looked at the now engrossed little group.

"Ah Helen Svensson nee Johnson" smiled Mary, "you really do look like your dad."

Adam stood forward and said "I am Adam Round and this is Mary Mustow my secretary!"

"I was just coming to meet our latest addition because you my lad are taking a huge load off my shoulders, and I am pleased to hand it over. Mary, on your computor accessed like this" she demonstrated "are a number of files and issues confronting our communications office of which you not I am the head," she grinned at Adam saying "call me over any issue, anything at all. Bye"

Off she went, and Mary mused that someone had just pulled the plank from beneath their feet and they were both hurtling towards the cold grey water.

Mary Mustow smiled and said to Captain Johnson "I suppose you and James worked your introduction as a little joke. I have read the books by Catherine and her Grandad and I never thought in a month of Sundays that I would ever meet any of you. I know this job is for the same employer but usually there are such a lot of employees that you scarcely get to know any of them. Well I have now met three of the top wallahs, on my first morning-- hey ho!"

"You could see a few others in the canteen you know!" said the Captain as he exited. The Whistler viewed all this from his spy camera system and could see that Mary was delighted but not really overawed." She will be a real addition" he thought, quietly humming.

Adam Round went through the files that Helen had placed for him on his computor. He read each one slowly and deliberately. Suddenly he punched the air with excitement and delight, startling Mary. "I knew I was right!"

James Whistler knew which file he had just read and was himself reading the latest medical bulletin on Heinrich Schmidt.

He lost himself in this bulletin and absent mindedly called "come in!" when he heard a knock at his door. Adam Round stood there with a smile so wide it threatened to reach his ears.

"You are a clever operator Mr. Whistler; you almost convinced me I was wrong. Almost, yes almost!"

"Now you have read the file what do you want to make public?"

Adam Round stood and thought "basically none of it. Now I am the other side of the fence I am staggered on how much my viewpoint has changed."

"Rumours will out and it is your job to scotch or nip in bud those rumours, so how would you do that?"

Adam Round thought for a moment and said "well now that really will be difficult. I suppose that we could offer an article on human health in Space and cover all of the illnesses that have been experienced on a mission by mission basis saying "Nothing to report" where there has been nothing to report we could fill in a vast and boring amount where there is something to report and simply say for the latest mission that there is nothing to report other then the mouse had a leg infection which seemed to heal quickly. We could finish by saying "watch this Space!" in fact we could serialise it so that the latest missions won't even go into print for several months yet but it would give us a platform for discussion,"

"Ok said the Whistler, for the moment you will get away with that but your face will become known and then one day, a reporter is going to say 'how big an increase in intelligence do we get when we go to the other side'?"

"I think I will do my best to look stupid and ask if he recommends that I go there myself."

Next I think I will try to look as if I've never heard that said and ask why on earth does he think that has happened, after all I am just the press release officer" and then when the reporter pursues me further I will wave my arms wildly in the air and say "quadrupled!"

I would expect to get a laugh with that, and perhaps the reporter would challenge me about the mouse and my answer would be "The mouse. Yes he is cute little thing but in spite of intense questioning he has told me nothing!"

Perhaps I would then say "Any more questions while we are on the topic?"

"Ok not bad, nodded James, "but if that scenario does occur take Heinrich with you and he can say how his debriefing which is still ongoing has given him so much time on his hands that there is a marked improvement in his snooker and his darts!

That really does appear to have happened by the way.

I think I will ask the Prof to sit in on your first press session and he is the master in such situations, he can defuse an angry mob with a few well chosen words and you could do well to learn from him."

"I thought the Prof had retired but if you do fetch him over please don't forget that Mary would never forgive me if she wasn't introduced!"

Adam Round returned to his office and Mary looked expectantly at him. "Well show us where the canteen is then!" they locked the office with Mary just remembering to switch on her recorded standby message as they went in search of food. Mary went in the queue for hot food and stared back at a woman who was staring at her. "Did James tell you to mention his name?" asked Nancy Wisdom.

Mary smirked guiltily "he did, he said you might not serve me if I didn't mention it Nancy."

Nancy smiled and said "well in this age with faster than light travel, news of your arrival reached our ears three days ago!"

"Yes I suppose that is just about as impossible as everything else I have seen this morning. Fish and Chips please!" Nancy Wisdom smiled and knew she had made a friend Mary Mustow thanked her lucky stars especially when she got to the pay desk and found this first meal was on the house. As she made her way back to Adam's table she caught the eye of Eric Whistler and he winked at her just as she recalled who he was. She glowed with pleasure. She said to Adam "I feel like Oliver Twist in Mr. Brownlow's house after living in with Fagin!" Adam barely reacted and she could see he was mulling over what he had learnt that morning.

She ate her lunch with relish.

CHAPTER 26

THE SPACE CENTRE HOLDS A HEAD TO HEAD TO DISCUSS TIME TRAVEL

James Whistler knew that a bit of brainstorming would probably flush out the real results of their present knowledge. He invited Judder, Heinrich, Captain Johnson and Eric Whistler, Helen and Henrik, Smed, and then as an afterthought Adam Round and Mary Mustow.

Fast forward now a few days to the actual meeting, The Whistler asked Mary to polish her secretarial skills and take shorthand notes. He knew hardly anyone else would be able to read shorthand, and he privately thought the only other thing that could improve security was if everyone spoke Welsh. This was an idle muse, but it still struck him that it would make penetration of their records very, very difficult.

Mary sat with pencil poised above her notepad and the Whistler began.

"Gentlemen, we have probably achieved something very close to our goal. On our side of the rethe we had already concluded that due to the inverse time function of the transition from real time into the rethe we could stretch and compress time. By an unbelievable fluke the time decided upon by Captain Johnson hit the one rethe time which is neutral. There is no compression or extension of time. Some of our Space missions though have had considerable extension or a small compression of time and we still haven't really explained that yet. We do not know of the mechanism by which the unwanted extensions and compressions occur.

We were correct in our conclusion that no matter what we did, time still moved inexorably forward, in our world.

The latest mathematics in which time is considered an imaginary axis, shows that whenever we visit the other side then time could just possibly run the other way.

Our first unmanned mission had a visitor on board and this mouse came through unscathed. Our second mission had a man on board, and he came through ok.

What you don't know is that the mouse had a bad swelling on his one leg, but it had gone completely when he returned.

Heinrich here heard a rumour to that effect and having just been diagnosed with suspected cancer, he volunteered. Heinrich appears to have been cured, but possibly even more significant that that, his mental focus has improved!"

Mary Mustow paused in her scribbling and glanced back over her work. Yes! She was easily fast enough to do it! She waited for the Whistler to continue.

James Whistler drew breath, "I have gone over the data from the mouse trip and there were two possibly significant differences between that and the Heinrich trip. There is one obvious difference and that concerns the shriek. The mouse trip did not record a shriek. The mouse trip also only fired rockets once to get back into the rethe from the other side.

The only conclusion that I have been able to draw from this is that though it was factored in, we did not get it right. What did we not get right? The effect of a human body being positive mass that's what. There was no mass factored in for the mouse trip, and yet there was no shriek. The mouse of course is thousands of times lighter then a man, and was simply an insignificant mass. Something in the equations governing the balance between matter and antimatter is missing a link.

We have put ourselves in a better position than otherwise we might have. We sent a human over to the other side. That is an argument we can use against the animal rights nutters, after all we deliberately sent a man but the mouse sneaked on the ship of its own free will. Now perhaps it is necessary to use mice, rats, dogs or whatever until we find out what went on when Heinrich went over! If we are careful, we could also study the health issues more closely and try to determine whether there is a benefit or a threat."

"Is it true that you had been diagnosed with cancer, Heinrich?" asked Captain Johnson.

"My medical records have been sequestered and are now a closely guarded document!" replied Heinrich, "But you can take it from me that it is true. My specialist was so shocked when he examined me that he openly said it was as if he had looked at the wrong scans when he made the original diagnosis."

In so far as a human's own senses allow me to tell what went on: I did get an uncomfortable pain in my back that started as I went through to the other side. After that I had too many wonders to observe to remember my own predicament. After I got back I suddenly felt as if a faint mist had been cleared from my mind and possibly due to being on sick leave, my snooker and darts capability has improved. I still feel clearer minded. It is a brand new sensation for me and I really do not have sufficient command of language, either English or German for that matter to give a truly apt description."

"How different was the sensation of exiting the rethe on the other side?" asked Eric Whistler.

"Quite honestly Eric, you would have to go through it yourself. It is different. The shuddering is similar and yet not the same and just before I got back, during the second rocket blast I got a sort of inside out view of the plughole effect!"

"I think we should use a trained squirrel!" said Smed. "A squirrel is an intelligent creature and we could perhaps devise a few exercises where he gets a food reward. We could detect his body rushing past an infra red detector to initiate the following stage of the process!"

"Well volunteered Smed!" grinned Eric Whistler.

"Now let's talk about time travel! James Whistler whetted his lips with his tongue.

"There was a subtle bit of decision making when constructing the automatic programme. From Henrik Svensson's speck of dirt we already now that we can stretch or even compress time on our side of the rethe. I programmed the total rethe time adding entrance to it from both our clockwise world and the anticlockwise world to be such that Heinrich would have reappeared on our continuum after about a week. However set against that was another calculation about what would happen to Heinrich whilst he was on the other side. This was an untried situation but Helen Svensson and I have burnt loads of midnight oil and we considered what to do. Our calculations proved spot on because Heinrich neither lost nor gained any nett time. Therefore Heinrich went backwards in time for about a week whilst he was on the other side. Just to keep the numbers easy we chose figures for our computor programme that resulted in a 162 hour time shift in both directions!"

Even Heinrich was stunned, but smiled as he realised he was in the history books, behind the mouse perhaps but still the first human.

"I am not given to histrionics" growled Heinrich, "But I must say I felt this absurd jealousy towards the mouse, when I realised he had beaten me to it. This was such a ludicrous thought, and was so out of character, that I immediately ignored it but thinking about it now, if I had been a weak minded person would I have been so overcome with jealousy that I couldn't function? It isn't a very nice thought you know!"

"Adam, have you thought any more about how to present our findings to the world?"

"I have thought of very little else! My view now is that my original idea on presenting a series of articles describing all health issue is I feel sure the best way forward. I will write articles based on Catherine Whistler's archive records, and I propose to keep the wording in layman's language. I will not compromise my honesty but on any sensitive issue I will come to those on the top floor for advice! I think that the jealousy issue may turn out to be a frightening one. What would have happened to the Mule or the Donkey if they had experienced such a thing? Instinct tells me that it would not be good. I trust your health will remain ok Heinrich and when my articles catch up with the present day, I will come and find you, for further thoughts."

"Did you----? "started James Whistler.

"Every word!" answered Mary.

"Ok this meeting is at a close. Should any one have further thought please bring them to my attention." James Whistler relaxed and the various wallahs in there helped them selves to coffee, while they chatted amongst themselves.

James Whistler was surprised when Mary Mustow took her typed version of events to him, two days later.

"Mr. Whistler, I struggled with the after lecture chatter but I think I got most of it!"

The Whistler turned to the last couple of pages and read them. Mary had somehow remembered and shorthanded all of the chatter that went on during the final cup of coffee.

"How on earth did you get all this down?" he marvelled.

"You ought to be in an editorial meeting. There is often more than one person talking at a time and I was always expected to get it all down, and I just developed a skill for it."

James Whistler was not a man given to swearing, but he just ejaculated "Prat!" as he thought of her erstwhile editor.

Mary laughed saying "it is so nice when someone really does appreciate my skills!"

Back in her own office, Mary decided to take an early lunch. She knew Adam Round would be deeply into his health in Space issues. So she switched her office phone over to its 'gone for lunch' message.

In the canteen Nancy Wisdom was talking earnestly to a man of about her own age and introduced Jarvis Kellar, 'my young man'.

Jarvis went through the pleasantries of introduction and then took his meal to the pay kiosk. Nancy Wisdom grinned at Mary. "You look like a cat with two tins of cream!"

"It is so nice to be appreciated for your work. Why I ever put up with that editorial skunk for so long I will never know. Steak and kidney pie please."

Nancy suddenly said "We shall have to find you a boyfriend!"

"There is a nice thought "Who have you got in mind?" Nancy had to admit that there wasn't any body suitable that she could think of but grinning, promised to keep her eyes and ears open.

Mary slid her tray towards the pay kiosk and said "I won't hold my breath then! But suddenly stopped in her tracks and said "Who is that?"

"Ah" said Nancy with a gleam in her eye. "I had forgotten him, that's Doctor Barry!"

Mary had read Catherine's books and she had idly wondered what he was like. There were quite a number of characters with photos in the book but Doctor Barry was not amongst them.

Mary sat at the next table and Doctor Barry surprised her by saying "hello Mary Mustow! Don't be surprised, there isn't a person in the Space service who hasn't heard of your exploits!" seeing the shear disbelief on her face he grinned and admitted varnishing the truth, "just a little poetic licence!" he intoned in his scholarly way.

"My exploits!" she laughed, "I didn't nearly kill Fordy!" as she said that she suddenly remembered the first telephone call from Don Ford but she only just made the connection. "I have actually had a conversation with a man that you shot!"

After lunch Mary left first and Doctor Barry grinned as she patted her hair into place whilst passing a mirror. "She hasn't given up yet!" he thought. The thought made him smile.

CHAPTER 27

JANE JOHNSON HAS A THOUGHT, AND JUDDER HAS ANOTHER

Jane was still helping Catherine Whistler and was even keener now that she actually got paid for doing something that she had come to love.

"Do you know Catherine I think this time travel lark is proving to be a lot more difficult to grasp than I ever thought. All of the stories ever written about it seem to have a calendar and you just dial in the date and there you go, and you arrive somewhere other than the present. But I can see a problem!"

"So can I, but you first!"

"Well when we enter the rethe from our side we have found we can compress time or stretch time but it always goes forward. You can get stuck in the rethe and time whizzes by at its normal speed. When you exit the rethe you may find six or seven weeks have gone by as Henrik did with his famous decimal point that was actually a spec of dirt. This means that you can get into a situation where time passes you by. When you come back to reality time has gone by and there is no way back. You are stuck where you are in our time continuum.

It strikes me that the exact opposite is likely to happen when on the other side of the rethe and time will go backwards. Let us say that you spend an amount of time there equating to a week in our zone, then you would have gone back a week. Now when you come back to our side provided Helen's equations are factored in correctly you would probably come out last week. So we may have a method of going back in time but at some natural rate, just as we can go forward at some natural rate. The thing is I don't see that we can freely go from one to the other by which

I mean if you want to go into the future you have to be on our side and wait for it to arrive, and if you want to go into the past you have to be on the other side and wait for it to arrive.

If we go into the past and emerge say 10 years ago, will we have that peculiar writhing existence seen in the two bars experiment? I am going to chat this over with Kingdom."

"I'm glad you went first Jane and no mistake! I have thought along similar lines but I never quite made the same connections as you seem to have done. It could be very interesting; because we may be able to venture into the past far enough to find out what went on in ancient china, for sake of argument. If we could escape back to our own lifetime without causing old age deaths amongst the crews we could fill a number of historical blanks!"

"We shall definitely need the big brains on this one, because it seems to me that to go ten years into the past we are going to have to go on a ten year mission! Helen has the distinction of being the one who clearly surmised the properties of the rethe, and we have used them to effectively shift matter faster than light it seems. Yet we do not go faster than light it is just that our exit point is reached by travelling through a region where time does not in itself exist. I must talk to her about the possible dynamics of what exactly is going on. The rethe seems to me to be an extremely narrow interface and has a zero time element because the clockwise Space time continuum on one side is exactly balanced by the anticlockwise Space time continuum on the other side. I think that research direction is irrevocably changed because time travel being a nice concept is probably useless, but the reordering of cell structures caused as you jump across the rethe and out the other side, will have a profound affect on the few who can afford to fund a jump for themselves, particularly if they are terminally ill. As an aside I can't entirely rid my mind of the 'groundhog day' syndrome, so we must proceed with caution.

No doubt in the near future we will find out a little more of what happened to Heinrich. He says he is now clearer minded, so is he younger? Has his intelligence been improved? Has his character integrity been compromised? There are some mighty issues arising. Will the mouse live longer and if he does will Heinrich also do that? Has the disease cure actually been due to journeying through the rethe or has it been from sitting inside the gravity motor control fields?"

Catherine Whistler had already considered some of Jane's points but she contented herself by saying "Hmmmmm!"

Just at the time that this was going on, Judder was sitting down to a meal and suddenly found himself coughing as he almost choked.

"What on earth is the matter with you?" asked Nadine offering him a glass of water.

"I think I know why we have the time travel discrepancies on our missions!" spluttered Judder.

Nadine smiled and said "well I know I won't understand but enlighten me!"

"Well the rethe is vast and it is the border between matter and anti matter existences. The thing is, penetration from one side to the other occurs naturally. I know this because it explains Sonny and FB1. So due to the vastness of the rethe, penetrations are going on in a random manner all the time, and if we happen to be in there while a random action is in progress, then it can affect our exit time. I am sure that this is right and it would explain why there doesn't seem to be a simple law to account for it. We are affected by random goings on that we are blissfully unaware of! I think I'll bounce this idea of dad and see what he thinks."

"Sounds reasonable to me!" smiled Nadine, "Now finish your breakfast!"

Brian did just that and then thought some more.

"Yes, the rethe is vast but because the time and other normal dimensions are effectively zeroed, it is as if the rethe is simultaneously microscopic. It means that any ship that is in there will feel the effect of other random reactions going on. When we go into the rethe it is not chemical but it is a physical reaction. If some other action is going on, it may be light years away in our world terms, but we would still feel it. If the reaction was a big one it could add years to our space flight whereas if the reaction was the other way it could compress our time in the rethe to virtually nothing. I think I may ask for another party!"

He rang the Prof and placed his notion before him. The Prof grinned with delight and said "I think you should ask for another party!"

CHAPTER 28

THE NEXT PARTY WAS HELD AT THE JOHNSON'S

In one of the more unusual moments the Prof decided he would like Liz to see something of the other's houses and was prepared to put up with the inevitable tiring journey.

They duly arrived at the Johnson's and found this house to be quite as grand as one may expect from the premier space captain of the day.

One by one the folk arrived and as they were all expecting dinner, the arrivals all happened within a half hour.

Kingdom Johnson was an American but he had developed a palate that favoured the good old roast dinners popular in the UK.

When all his guests were seated, Jane marched in pushing quite the largest hostess trolley ever seen and carefully placed the first meal in front of the Prof. He looked at the meal and realised it was hard to tell the difference between it and one he may have served up himself.

Jane grinned confidently at him saying "tuck in to those runner beans, they are a speciality of mine!"

The grinning Prof had to admit that they were at least as good as his own and generously said so.

Kingdom Johnson smiled a rather guilty smile and apologised. "Sorry Prof but I diverted a few of those meant for stellar two!"

The Prof said nothing but a sort of satisfaction showed on his face. Jane Johnson had cooked the entire meal herself but admitted that she had watched the Prof whenever she had the chance and so it was agreed by all, that she had equalled the Prof. She felt overwhelmed by a sort of smug delight. Jane let it be known that she had invited Heinrich, who was expected to bring Venus, and her brother Rod, who may well be accompanied he had said, and they were due in the following day.

As was the form at all of these dos, the first day was spent catching up with family and friendly gossip. The Johnsons had a large garden quite different in character to the Prof's but big enough for some good healthy rough and tumble for the children.

Jane suddenly realised that Hannah Jackson would be missing along with her husband due to other commitments.

"I shall miss her when it comes to organising bed time!" she thought. However about an hour later when answering the front door bell, she was delighted to welcome them in.

"I thought you couldn't make it, and I was just realising I would miss Hannah at children's bed time. Come in, come in!"

"Hello reverend, have you come to make sure that we don't forget about God in our deliberations?" smiled Kingdom Johnson.

"Hello Kingdom, I might have a few words with Jane on that, because she gives me food for thought you know!"

"Well all that will have to wait until tomorrow when we get down to business, today is purely social!"

They heard the strains of 'what a swell party this is' and both grinned. Jane had sufficient in the way of leftovers to provide her late guests with a full meal, the reverend fairly smacking his lips as he tucked in.

The evening passed as all previous parties, and breakfast the following morning. passed much the same as all the parties held at the Prof's place. At around ten o'clock Kingdom Johnson called the meeting to order and invited Judder to set the ball rolling.

Judder stood and cleared his throat, just as a knock came on the front door. Kingdom Johnson welcomed the new guest in and it was none other than Rod, his rescuer from a difficult situation during the Donkey's era. Rod was hungry so Kingdom took him out to the breakfast bar and showed him where everything was and left him to it.

Judder was just getting to the nub of his latest idea.

"It struck me suddenly that we were looking too hard for a solution to the time anomalies, and after all we had had the answer shoved into our faces without realising it at the time."

The audience was quietly expectant.

"When FB1 came hurtling at us, both Eric Whistler and Henrik Svensson noticed the system paralysis we get when we are close to a portal. We were not that close to a portal although we were just in the process of entering one but we were very close to FB1. I believe that FB1 and Sonny are bridges that go right through their own portal and out the other side not into but through the rethe and into the negative matter existence.

This gateway gives rise to a continuous exchange but galactically speaking on a microscopic scale. The reaction self sustains but is nowhere near enough to generate conditions for a big bang. The matter and anti-matter hurtle towards each other then neutralise as they each swallow one another up, making heat in the process. I believe that the portals are so narrow as to confine the size of the reaction so that the reaction just sustains and doesn't get out of control as would be the case for a big bang.

Now I do not believe that Sonny and FB1 are alone. I believe that there are many such occurrences some of which are stable like Sonny and FB1 and some are not. The unstable ones will exist for a spell of time and if we are in the rethe simultaneously, they will affect our time by an incalculable, random amount.

I am as you know a duffer at maths but there are those here who may just find a way of bringing some control into the situation." He sat down.

The Prof was away with the fairies again and the Whistler had resumed his robot man expression.

Jane Johnson stood and said "Judder I think you may just have stolen my thunder!"

She smiled and commented further "it was unfortunate that the word rethe which was ether spelt backwards was used to describe the no man's land between positive and negative existences as it would surely have been more appropriate to describe 'the other side' so to speak. My own thoughts which I was wishing to present to this meeting are so nearly exactly what Judder has postulated that I don't really think I can add any more just now, well not on the time travel issue."

She thought for a moment then added "Helen somehow divined that there was an inverse law with regard to the apparent time involved. Now we have had sufficient experience to show that her idea was sound, what we do not know is *why* this law seems to exist, and this may be tied up with a companion law applicable to entities getting into the rethe from the other side. If we can propose a notion which encompasses both sides so to speak then we may be able to say which way the balance of matter transfer was during these random activities and so get a handle on just what is happening.

However I think at the moment that we are effectively stuck with a possibility of stretching or compressing time but no matter which side of the rethe we operate from time in general will go at its preordained rate, forward for us and backwards for the little green men on the other side.

From a humanitarian viewpoint I would like to see the medical side of things pursued and perused much more deeply. We know that it is possible to straighten out a minor defect in a human being or an animal and we also know that there is an effect on the mind as Heinrich would testify. Would it be possible to relieve dementia for example?" perhaps we should refocus our efforts, and look into such possibilities, but if we do we are going to have to proceed carefully.

No one has explained to me what would have happened to Heinrich's mission if his ship collided with some small particles of negative matter and I think a lot more research with unmanned missions is required." She sat down.

"Good on yer sis!" bawled out Rod from the back row. Jane shot out of her seat and embraced her brother, "I never noticed you sorry Rod!"

"Jane yer make a mean bacon sarnie!" he chuckled, "and have yer met me wife yet?"

Jane broke off from her embrace thinking "wife?" to see a fit looking young woman standing by the door of the breakfast bar. Her face split into an enormous grin as she took the outstretched hand.

"Esmeralda known as Essie, glad ter meet yer Jane!"

The door chimes rang out and Kingdom was wondering where the hell Essie had come from but he was nearest so he opened the door and welcomed Heinrich and Venus.

He looked at them and asked "Are you two stepping out?"

Heinrich smiled and looked at Venus who sighed saying "Well I suppose we can't keep it a secret any longer so yes we are!"

Heinrich follow me!" requested Kingdom Johnson, "here you are, view this recorder it will bring you up to date!"

Heinrich studied the disc player for a few minutes and then nodded.

The Whistler had been back out of his trance for a few minutes now and commented, "Those two little speeches have showered us scientists with an unparalleled amount of work. I hope Helen can solve the issues of the balanced existences because I shall be too busy to help her! It strikes me that Sonny and FB1 may be safety valves between the rethe and the other and allow an exchange as a means of maintaining an exact balance between the two sides."

`Heinrich asked "if I were to go on a second mission to the other side would I regain the problem that I lost?"

James Whistler was silent for a moment. "No, I think that every thing in that transfer became a little better ordered but I have wondered if a bar of metal with a crack in it would be healed, so there are many, many things like that, that we can do with unmanned missions. We must try all those before we send another explorer mission there."

Venus, who was stood at Heinrich's side listening, let out a gasp of relief.

James Whistler smiled at her kindly. "Heinrich is our most experienced away team leader and had shown his worth on every mission. We don't want to lose him any more then you do and I give you permission Heinrich, to explain to Venus why you volunteered for that last mission."

Heinrich took Venus to a quiet corner and explained his reasons for volunteering but swore her to secrecy. "You must tell no-one not even your mom or dad!" and then he explained why such security was necessary.

"OK I understand, after all my mom and dad pulled a right stunt to make sure I was born on mars. I lived there until I was eight and then went back when I was sixteen so I understand the occasional need for secrecy, but swear to me now that you will never lie to me!"

Heinrich grinned and agreed that he would be truthful at all times. He then asked why she had decided to come back to earth and Venus told him that she fancied life on earth, and got a job as a baby sitter and anyway was fed up of her mars nickname of 'Queenie' and so here she was.

James Whistler said "I wish I had invited Adam Round and Mary Mustow to this do, because there could be a lot for him to think about and Mary is so skilled at short hand that it would be the quickest and most secure way to get archive reports off to Catherine. You know if Judder is right and I think he is, then once we have an open bridge such as Sonny, we can move it to where ever we like. These bridges are like fish that are waiting to be caught. Perhaps we should initiate research into how we could find a harvestable one, or even see if we can build one. If we could do that we could invigorate all sorts of otherwise cold places such as Titan. It might be cheaper than building a nuclear power station."

Those in the room suddenly looked glum as the import of the discoveries hit them. They all knew that it would take years of research to cover even half of the avenues now opening up.

Helen suddenly smiled. "Jane was right when she said it was unfortunate that I called the boundary existence the rethe, because it would have been an excellent word to describe the other side. However I plan to add to my thesis as follows. Firstly our space is the ether secondly the transition from the ether to the rethe will remain named exactly so. We are too far entrenched in the notions of it all now to bring about confusing changes. I have decided to call the negative space time continuum the 'other' and just for good measure if transition from the other into the neutral zone has any unusual properties I have decided that it should be called the retho, other backwards. So now we have the 'ether' into the 'rethe/ retho' and then from there to the 'other' and back again! Objections anyone!"

Heinrich was now up to speed with the goings on and cleared his throat as he stood.

"For those of you who don't know, Venus and I are an item. He dipped his head in acknowledging the smiles that went about the room.

"Now Jane mentioned the medical research possibilities and as you all know, Venus was conceived and born on Mars and has shown herself to be normal in every sense. We have had an instance where a mouse got onto an unmanned mission and seems to have been cured of an ailment.

Following that I myself went on the next mission with a minor ailment and so far it has gone and has shown no sign of coming back. The exact nature of my complaint is classified but I think if word of it gets out the space centre will be inundated with curious and downright unhelpful wallahs all wishing to go on a mission. Without doubt this will raise huge moral and ethical issues and we must have some carefully thought out strategy to inure ourselves against inappropriate use of our resources. For me myself the experience was strange. It made me feel in some way better ordered and clearer minded.

I gather that going through into the other somehow sort of set all my parameters to default and like many a computer I have benefitted from the experience. I wonder whether an old man going through might just come out somewhat younger.

Perhaps a baby born with a defect may get straightened out. Anyway whatever the pros and cons of the situation I believe that research should quietly continue and we can build up a dossier of effects on various problems. I further think that mankind may consider us derelict in our duties if we do not dig further into these matters! The one thing we could do using sick animals is to place them inside our double sphere ship, and go through a cycle of operating the gravity shield system and see if it is that that has effected ailment cures.

With regard to keeping this knowledge secret, this may be difficult. Adam Round had already pretty well guessed the truth, so we are fortunate that he has thrown his lot in with us, but no doubt some other newshound will uncover it sooner rather than later. Now if anyone has any suggestion for a smoke screen will he or she please communicate their idea to Adam Round, but make sure you use a secure scrambled phone line!"

Heinrich sat down to another round of total silence as his words sank home.

Note from Catherine Whistler: It suddenly struck me that we might have squeezed a few more years into Grandad's life if we had had just a little more knowledge when he did his space trip. I am sure that Heinrich is right, but it can surely only be a matter of time before people are clamouring to go on a trip.

Judder suddenly interjected saying "we could acknowledge that cures do seem part of the jump through process but only with a single occupant on board the ship otherwise we could claim there would be a real danger of inter mixing the DNA, with catastrophic results such as fly and man mixed, as in the sci-fi film about that. Any such mission would have to be exactly as Heinrich's one and the whole thing would be automatically controlled by on board computors. The biggest danger would be the effect of other unstable bridges like FB1 causing time lapses of several years. Such things are beyond our control and with a few more 'facts' like that, the number of volunteers is likely to be pared to a minimum! It has also occurred to me before these discussions, and my thought train is in line with Heinrich's and Jane's notions that the rethe penetration ship has an outer shield and not a core, and as a necessity the pilot and possible passengers have to sit inside the control fields. It is possible that these control fields are responsible for the improvement in bodily cell order."

It went silent for a few moments before Jane quietly added "we could try experiments in the jump ship using sick animals without going through the rethe! We could remove the diamond tube and its contents and simply go through a training procedure involving opening and closing the gravity shield systems and log any health changes that occur, if any!"

The Prof smiled ruefully as he muttered to himself that he had unfortunately been born a few years too early. He knew that he still had the intellect to be useful, but he also knew that his body no longer had the stamina and he was saddened by this little truth.

The Whistler had been quiet for some time but he suddenly stood, saying "I consider we have several serious branches of research here that must be done separately but simultaneously. Firstly we must study the FB1 portal and see what is happening on the other side. For example we know we get heat on our side, so does the other side have heat as well or is it a cold radiation. Can we draw inferences that tell us whether or not that there is a mini black hole there?

For security we should consider doing the medical research on mars, and we might consider moving the diamond shard business to mars as well leaving only the security of the deliveries at risk and some one else can handle that. I thank the Johnson's for their hospitality and suggest we slowly filter out of here and get back to reality!" he sat down and was gratified to hear the urgent buzz of conversation as the various delegates considered these late suggestions. The delegates slowly went about their own business but it was several days before Rod and Essie took their leave.

Note from Catherine Whistler: I think Jane and I will have our hands full for the foreseeable future. I haven't told any one yet but Eric and I are expecting what I hope will be our last family addition, I noticed that Venus has shown more than a passing interest in our archiving work so I think I will sound her out and see if she would be interested in joining our archive team, but first I will approach the Whistler to see what salary I could offer her.

The Whistler said nothing over the next few days but he was mulling over another concept in the back of his mind. He acknowledged that the way the present understanding stood, there was no way to simply jump time zones and yet he could not rid himself of the notion that whilst in the rethe your cocoon was existing in a virtually dimensionless place, where time had no kingdom. He further considered that this being the case it was how you exited with your cocoon that determined exactly where in real time you rejoined existence either in the ether or the other and so surely there would have to be some means to decide just how when and where you would exit. For the moment you entered at some point in time, and exited somewhere else in time partly depending on what else was going on in the rethe whilst your cocoon was in there.

What would happen if you could ditch your cocoon whilst still in the rethe? Could you transfer from one cocoon to another?

He allowed his mind to wander along a path which suggested that the rethe had a static time value of one or unity. That is to say that the time was linked by ether time divided by other time. This was consistent with the inverse time notion because of the existence of a denominator and he wondered if that was the means by which the inverse time rule applied, after all if the time in the rethe was equal to one over some other value where the other value was the time allowed by a space captain whilst in the rethe then it would all fit. Of course it was then possible that the value required by transitioning from the other would follow a similar pattern and he wondered whether or not the fraction was the other way up with the unity constant being on the bottom instead of the top. As a transition was made from the ether to the other and back again; surely the two factors were exactly that and could be multiplied together to produce the effective nullification of time whilst in the border regions. This would explain a matter that had troubled him quietly for some time, and that was that when inside a cocoon time still existed in some form or other, thus permitting radio transmissions and other little quirks. It would also explain how the behaviour of a spaceship in its cocoon could have an influence on time when in a region so far considered to have no time.

During the ensuing month, trials were carried out and it was established beyond reasonable doubt that any healing process was due to going through the rethe into the other and back again. It had nothing to do with sitting inside the gravity masking fields of the spaceships used for the jump. It surely couldn't be long now before some newshound got a sniff of what was going on!

The Whistler considered his approach. He was going to follow his own lines of reasoning, then put his train of thought in front of Helen and after she had had time to digest and contribute he would place the notions before Judder and his dad.

The most exciting and yet troubling thought that had occurred to him was that the rethe may not be dimensionless but could be multi dimensional with the dimensions effectively cancelling each other out, thus appearing to be dimensionless overall. At the moment a reasonable theory had been constructed where our time zone ran in effect in antiparallel to the other which had negative time, and the interface between them had been termed the rethe. If you considered that the interface ran in effect as a north-south divide, was it not possible that there could also be an east-west or an up-down divide joining two other existences? If this was possible it may be that there were an infinite number of other existences? If there were other existences, surely the rethe had to be considered as a portal between them and was therefore the most important scientific entity ever conceived. Big thoughts!

CHAPTER 29

THINGS SIMMER MORE SLOWLY

The next few days saw a period when ideas stayed in the minds of those that were thinking them, though the Whistler did present his ideas to Helen Svensson. She saw immediately that he had explained the inverse time issue which she had decided upon based on empirical notions concluded from a study of gathered data.

Judder phoned up the Prof for a chat, then received the invite for a visit and took Nadine over the following day. Initially they were chatting about family issues which the Prof devoured greedily. The conversation veered from one topic to another but then Judder calmly mentioned that he was concerned about space travel.

Nadine heard what he said and immediately asked him to spit it out.

Judder drew a slow breath and said "well it's about the rethe," he sighed "as you know dad, I'm not a scientist but after that party just the other day I couldn't help wondering if we have been proceeding blindly thinking that we are on the right path when in actual fact we are on a single path that is only one of a number of paths that could well be legion. Should we ever fall from our path of righteousness, so to speak we could find ourselves in a situation that has no precedent and I fear many people could be lost!"

The Prof sat silent for a few moments then spoke "if I understand you correctly Brian, you are thinking that the rethe is not just an interface between our existence and the negative time existence, but is or may be an interface between an infinite number of other existences which may have incalculable effects on time, and furthermore since we likely don't yet have a handle on the laws of physics that these existences entail, we are taking a risk whenever we use the jump!"

"Well yes that's about it and yet I think the jump is safe enough because we are protected by some as yet undiscovered law of physics. I read an account somewhere of a seagoing ship that Einstein managed to send away somewhere and retrieve it, but that the entire crew were raving mad afterwards. I never established whether this was journalistic invention or true, but if there is any truth in it, that does mean that we must be far more cautious!"

"Agreed" horned in the Whistler who had just arrived.

The Prof shot to his feet to welcome his new arrivals, smiling graciously at Josie and nodding at James.

Turning he grinned at Judder saying "it was obvious from our little phone conversation the other day that you had something on your mind so I took a liberty or two and invited other interested parties!"

He surprised Judder by further revealing that he had recorded the day's proceedings so far, and he requested that the Whistler watch the disc without delay.

When the catch up had been completed Judder noticed Mary Mustow and Adam Round in the room.

"How long have you two been here?" he mumbled.

Suffice it to say that all interested parties were now up to speed.

Judder spoke again "now you've all heard my worry about the supposed Einstein experiment and knowing what I know about Heinrich Schmidt I found myself fretting about the madness issue. The thing is do any of you know if Einstein actually carried out the experiment?" he turned to face the Whistler.

James Whistler confirmed that he had also heard the rumour years ago but could shed no further light on the issue stating that the whole thing was hidden behind a heavy military security blanket and that both the mule and the donkey had each destroyed so many records that he doubted if the truth would ever be known. "It is up to us to try to find a safe path through our present field of endeavour, which increasingly seems like a quagmire!"

"I am pleased that Mary and I have been invited over, but why exactly are we here?" queried Adam Round.

James Whistler opened his palms and simply said "OK cards on the table."

His audience waited expectantly. He continued "I have kept generally quiet about things going on in my mind though I have mentioned my ideas to Helen Svensson. Frankly Judder you have started thinking about issues that have troubled me since the last party". *Over the next half an hour he expounded the thoughts covered at the end of the last chapter, so I won't go over it again. Catherine.*

"I have considered at length and in depth what we should do and I believe the following to be the wisest. The present use of the jump must continue remembering that it is the only way to get to Stellar 2. My view about the random time element as postulated by Judder has hardened as I think that he is correct. Helen has managed to factor an element into the equations so though we have no control over that element, at least we have some understanding of it.

Sooner rather than later the press or the mob will access our little world and they will make strenuous efforts to horn in. You, Adam will need to present a well reasoned argument mentioning the dangers of DNA mix up and madness and any other discouraging little facts that can be elicited from our knowledge. Be very careful in your presentation, do nothing that will feed their appetite, rather you must seek to dampen it.

All exploration missions into some of the newly perceived issues will have to be unmanned. Right now I don't have any idea how we might traverse into the possible legion of other existences, but perhaps we can ask Smed to think about it for a few weeks.

Mary was scribbling quickly but in a very relaxed way. The Whistler admired this old fashioned skill and was delighted with her progress. He had already decided to play a little game with her. He added "I understand that we have a volunteer for the next jump visit to Stellar 2; the space captain offering his services is Doctor Barry and I think he would be an excellent commander of the next visit whenever that may be."

He grinned hugely when he noticed Mary's pencil pause ever so briefly at the mention of Doctor Barry.

"Right I think we could all do with a few minutes break, ah is that the doorbell? Mary would you get that please?" fortunately he was standing close to Elizabeth and applied firm pressure to her shoulder as she made to rise.

Mary came back in with Doctor Barry.

Josie Whistler wagged an admonishing finger at her husband "James you are the limit! I know your little game! Why don't you leave well alone?"

Mary was not at all put out and she said "Oh I know all about this man. Space captain extraordinaire. Resistance fighter; captain of a ship gathering data from Sonny. Etc etc! Did you just set me up Mr. Whistler?"

"I am sure he did it with the best of intentions but he is already too late!" So chortled Doctor Barry in his inimitable scholarly way, "we had our first date last night!"

Mary smiled saying "my late husband was nothing like this man and I am surprised that I even like him because I would have thought from what I read about him in Catherine's books that he wasn't my type. There were no photos of him in the book. When I first saw him in the canteen I was a little taken with him and asked Nancy who he was. Well, not my type? How wrong can you be?"

The Whistler had listened to the latest scuttlebutt and had indeed tried to set her up when he heard details of the few moments in the canteen when they always seemed to take their lunches at exactly the same time.

Josie still wagging her forefinger added "really James you are a man of science, an intellectual, but your subtlety even makes Judder seem like a master politician!"

Judder smirked and commented how nice it was for someone else to be in the firing line for a change.

Doctor Barry was asked to view the disc of the meeting so far and he raised his eyebrows as he realised that right at that moment he was ahead of every other space captain in the service. His doctorate was in astro physics so he had a decent grasp of the issues at stake, he didn't quite have the Whistler's robot man stance but he was lost deep in thought for a minute or two. Finally he asked "what security level is the information that you have just given me?"

The Whistler grinned saying that it was the highest level, but Adam Round shaking his head asked if the canteen could be used for allowing a controlled leak.

He added "Doctor Barry could 'accidently' let slip a few well chosen morsels of information and we could use that source to feed confirmation of things that they already think they know of, but if we do that then the Ford brothers must be in on the plan!"

What sort of information are you considering?" asked Judder and the Whistler at the same time.

"An hour ago I was told to feed the mob but to be careful in so doing. I have thought of nothing else since that moment. I believe that the mob must be allowed to put two and two together so that they will believe their own sources of intelligence. I am worried that we may underestimate them and indeed we have already been guilty of that before now. By the way has anyone scanned this building? My motive is to protect the space service and to allow information to filter out into the outside world with a view to getting mob supporters to show themselves. The Fords can take care of them then. The information once leaked cannot be retracted as you know so it will have to be good otherwise our 'fans' out there will simply disbelieve.

Once newshounds get a sniff of something perceived as important there will be no let up, believe me if anyone knows that, I do."

Mary added quietly "when I type up my report if I were to title it "foreseen and real dangers in space travel outside the ether" a title such as that would attract unauthorised viewings I am sure. If I present the issues of madness, lost in space, burnt to a frazzle in the other due to galactic confusion caused by DNA mixings and anything else I can glean from this meeting, it could well be a cause for the mob or anyone else to reflect on the wisdom of their chosen path, if that path is to horn in on a mission."

"Ok Mary do exactly that and present your effort to Adam. Then Adam after you have had chance to make additions or deletions bring the story up to me and we will then try to reflect, then edit it to its final version. The canteen is a good place to let slip a rumour and we will have to trust that the mob or the press will find a way to view the report- but do not make it easy for them. Follow all security protocols."

The Ford brothers were informed of this plan and said nothing, but both could sense inherent dangers in the cat and mouse games that would surely follow.

Judder felt a certain sense of satisfaction when he realised that James Whistler had also worried about the same issues but had come up with an excellent explanation. Judder once again thought he could smell that the Whistler's theory was correct.

Three weeks after this Venus joined our little archiving team, and I spent almost the whole of the next month trying to teach her how the archiving system worked, leaving Jane on her own to cope with the daily archiving. Venus is a bright girl, but the archiving system is now so complex that she had difficulty assimilating the system into her head. Fortunately she stuck at it doggedly and slowly at first began to take a little of the load away from myself and Jane.

I now have no doubt that she will achieve full operational status and teaching her has also taught me that when I consider retiring, we will need students perhaps for as much as full three years to bring them up to speed. Right now I can not see a need for the archiving system to be further upgraded, but you never can tell. Catherine Whistler.

CHAPTER 30

SMED HAS A FEW THOUGHTS.

The Whistler briefed Smedley Tomlinson as widely as he could on the issues facing the space service technical boys. The particular focus that he wanted was to investigate whether or not there were many outlets from the rethe or just the two that had so far been experienced. Accordingly he spent the greater part of his instruction on that particular point. Smed knew what was expected of him and went to his office for a good thumb sucking session.

He mulled various notions over in his mind and rejected them all except one. He knew that he only had to find one more escape route from the rethe to prove possible existence of other differing routes.
He pondered this deeply on the basis that there definitely were other escape routes. All he had to do was to think of a way to align his rethe cocoon such that it was bound to go into one.

He knew that there was a powerful directional or vectorial force applied to a positive matter such that it was ejected from the rethe to whence it came. This was dictated by the laws of galactic balance. He also knew that Heinrich had found exiting then reaccessing the rethe somewhat problematic. There was the perceived shriek that was as yet unexplained.

The idea began to form in his mind that the basic barbell shape of the rethe buster as he thought of it only permitted a straight line action, that is to say the other was seen as being effectively in anti-parallel to the ether.

What if he could introduce an angle into the action of the rethe buster shuttle? How would he attempt this?

His first small experiment was to check out the possibility of coercing the ether/other energy interchange into a curve rather than a straight line. He asked for and got a grown diamond from the Triton mines that had a bubble at each end but the link being a quarter circle quadrant, instead of a straight line.

He involved the Whistler and in just a few months he had had a rethe buster ship constructed where the crew sat in bubbles at each end being exactly at right angles.

Dummies were used as a crew and the mission was sent off to look to enter the same portal as had Heinrich. The gravity shield motors were switched exactly the same and the new design promptly exited the rethe. On board cameras and recorders recorded time, the view, the noises, the shuddering effects and many other things the scientists were interested in; particularly those that so far only had a vague explanation.

Back in the space centre the mission controllers waited patiently with rising tension as they awaited the return of the mission to the normal space time continuum.

This did not happen and after four months the ship was glumly considered lost. There was undiluted joy when it reappeared in the ether after 18 weeks.

The data gathered was studied ferociously and the reason for the delay became apparent. The notion that there were other existences had been proved beyond any shadow of a doubt. The ship had a minute angular error on the effective right angle of the two barbells this was due to the shuddering being much greater than so far experienced on manned missions, and the forces involved caused miniscule structural distortion on the ship.

This small error had meant that the first home run had gone into another time dimension. The ship had an automatic seek and find arrangement and when this did not receive a deactivation code it just kept traversing across the rethe until finally it made it back into the ether. This only happened once the ship was finally aligned correctly for a re-entry into the ether, and the ship was almost out of rocket fuel.

The recorded severity of the shaking had increased with each little jump and it was fortunate that the ship had maintained sufficient structural integrity to have managed a home run in the end.

The conclusion drawn was that the right angle arrangement on its own was simply not strong enough being inherently weak. Smed theorised that a better solution would have been to split the system into three and have two 120 degree partitions. He proposed a triangular mirror at the central intersection that could reflect energy to either or both of the slave barbells. He further proposed that at each barbell point there were in fact two barbells one full of positive matter and the other full of negative matter. Each barbell sphere would have a controlled gravity shield and the desired sphere could be opened up at the desired 120 degree point. The gravity fields of the companion barbells would be controlled such that both negative and positive matter could be exposed to a greater or lesser degree thus allowing the effective overall picture to be vectorially controlled so that an infinite variety of mass angles was available.

In addition to this each barbell ball end would have a carbon fibre tube connecting it to each of the other barbells so that a light but exceptionally strong structure would result.

This was tried and was proven effective and the superior structural integrity of this arrangement led to rapid advances in handling the jumps in and out of the rethe.

Smed was pleased with himself and the Whistler was delighted. He and Helen had burnt much midnight oil expanding their new branch of mathematics.

Whilst in and out of the rethe the ships could arrive in different space time continua easily but the efforts at garnering data were always neutralised when returning the ether. So in spite of all the success the basic goal of straight time travel remained elusive.

The greatest practical advance in space travel occurred during these experiments with the discovery of the anomalous occurrence detector.

Remember the diamond shard colour issue? Well these shards would pulse light when in the rethe if there was a large disturbance to the rethe from elsewhere. The colour and frequency were related to the size and time effect. The red pulsing indicated time compression and the blue pulsing indicated time extension, whereas the pulse frequency was analogous to the disturbance size. Space explorers could now use this information and compute to realign their exit vector according to the relative strengths of the barbell masking fields and could jump into another dimension, giving due allowance for the rethe distortion to settle. In this way it was predicted that the unwanted time errors could be reduced to insignificant proportions.

So far the space ship engineers have managed to construct barbell ships that would carry a crew of about 150. There seems little hope at the moment of making a ship in this format to rival the size of the Moneybag or even the Freeloader, but they are bigger than a shuttle yet still small enough to be stowed on board one of the larger vessels.

Smed pondered the information now at his disposal. He knew a ship could jump time zones and could be made to exit the rethe in other existences. He also knew that as soon as the return journey was done any time jump achieved was simply negated by the return journey. All of the missions into the unknown time had been unmanned though again a small rodent with a skin growth was included in the last mission but on return the growth had increased dramatically.

The Whistler and Heinrich had discussed this point at some length and though the germs of possible explanations were there, no-one so far had a verifiable explanation.

Smed asked for another sick rodent experiment to be tried out but in this instance the first jump was to be straight to the other. After re-entry to the rethe, then a sideways jump to other existence zones was organised and then re-examination back in the laboratory revealed that this rodent had a reduction in the size of its tumour- but it had not gone.

Smed wrote a detailed report and gave this directly to the Whistler. James Whistler read it thoroughly from end to end and found himself in agreement with Smed's conclusions.

The issues raised were truly legion but there was an irrefutable string of logic to the ailment cure section and that was that journeying in time could just as easily cause problems as cure them.

Heinrich read of this conclusion in due course. He found himself sweating at the thought that in stead of curing him, his mission could have killed him. Ignorance had truly been bliss.

The final line of Smed's report requested that manned missions be tried next as a matter of urgency but that all personnel involved would have to undergo a rigorous vetting including a total health screening.

Note from Catherine Whistler. I do not know how much longer I will be able to interpret these goings on as they are becoming more and more technical. I have striven to keep to Grandad's original notion, which was to put the adventures into plain language. The matters are now inextricably entwined in techno-jargon and it really is no longer easy to express the ideas in plain layman's words. In a moment of introspection I had to acknowledge inwardly that it is probably all getting beyond me, but I have discussed this entire last chapter at length with Jane and Venus. Hopefully the reader will still be able to glean the basics.

CHAPTER 31

THE WHISTLER HAS TO MAKE A DECISION

I found a request in my E-mail this morning asking if I would attend a meeting at the space centre for a discussion. When I got there I was issued with a security pass for the day and I walked in to a meeting that had a full house of interested parties.

James Whistler smiled and asked me to run over the latest chapter in my space story.

"Come on Catherine give it your best shot!" smiled Jane Johnson.

I went over it from memory and began to speak finishing with my conclusion about the difficulties in understanding just what was going on.

"Thank you Catherine" began the Whistler, "You may be pleased to know that we top scientists and engineers are struggling much the same as yourself, so don't give up just yet!"

Helen Svensson was nodding her agreement and the Whistler continued.

"As you know the space centre is not short of funds at the moment, but if we rush blindly on I think our purse will rapidly empty. I have studied all of the most recent data and I believe that we can jump time. Unfortunately such journeys can only be one way. If we consider sending an away team into a future time zone for example, the mission would have to await events there to unfold at the natural rate, and it could be years before anything significant were to happen. If they were then to attempt a return journey armed with whatever knowledge they had gleaned, I do not think that the time passed would simply be recouped so that they could slot back into their previous existence. I think that their bodies would have aged, and possibly at a quite different rate to ours so that they could re-arrive in our ether to find that they were so old as to be in danger of imminent death, or conversely find that none of us were still alive to welcome them back. I think this would effectively nullify any good that may otherwise have been achieved.

I propose therefore to stop all research into time travel forthwith!"

Helen Svensson's face said it all. Total utter relief.

Kingdom Johnson was slowly nodding as he looked across at the reaction from Eric Whistler.

Eric Whistler sniffed, sighed, nodded his head in an angled way and said that he was glad to be divested of the chance of leading such a mission. The Whistler was however not finished.

He reached behind his desk and flicked a switch. Several mobiles in people's pockets all began beeping as they lost their connection.

"Just a little security device fitted two days ago on the suggestion of the brothers Ford." He began acknowledging the smiles on the Ford brothers' faces.

"I do think that the only research should be confined to jumps in and out through to the other and back, not for time travel purposes but for medical reasons."

He then outlined in great detail what had happened to Heinrich, and this was news to quite a few in the room.

"I tell you this because it underlines why I think this branch of research should be followed up. This information is of the highest priority and I have had to review the security level of a number of you. Those who have had an upgrade will receive a suitable hike in remuneration levels but there will be no additional details in your personnel files except those held off site in the Ford's private vault system. This is so that there will be a minimum of information for any spies to pounce on.

We will attempt to pass off the news blackout that I just imposed as an experimental test, so hopefully this will be perceived as just another annoying security device.

Ok, meeting over please all return to your posts except Adam Round Mary Mustow, and the space captains. Oh and perhaps Judder and the Prof would like to hang around for a while."

The Whistler hit the door release and the others all trooped out. I was the last to exit but was stopped dead in my tracks by the Whistler's restraining arm.

"Don't worry Catherine I just didn't want the others to know that I was keeping you for a little longer!"

Mary Mustow had been scribbling furiously and when asked replied "three hours!"

"Ok Catherine expect Mary's report in about three hours, off you go now and find Jane and whoever in the canteen!"

This time as I left the office I found myself face to face with Josie Whistler. James Whistler waived her away and she knew that he would forgo the office cleaning routine this morning so she linked arms with me and we stalked off to the canteen. Jane was rattling to Nancy Wisdom and ordered two more cups of tea as we walked in. Back in the Whistler's office Judder claimed that he knew the reason for the shriek as returns to the ether were made when there was a mismatch of positive and negative masses.

"I think we are tearing time as the cocoon knows where it should eject us but the mass levels are trying to distort the picture resulting in that god awful ear splitting shriek!"

"Judder that is the first explanation offered for that phenomenon so I will give that due consideration!" nodded the Whistler.

"There is something else on my mind" added Judder, "you know how all data gathered when in another space time continuum is lost as we return to the ether?" he paused "well what if we disconnect all of the storage media before we return?"

The Whistler smiled ruefully and said "we already tried that but the natural laws always seem to get the better of us!"

"Ok then that really does seem to be that!" grinned Judder.

CHAPTER 32

MEDICAL RESEARCH

James Whistler knew that he would need to change the balance of his team somewhat just to cope with this realignment of his research thrust.

The Prof suggested that he advertise for a research candidate qualified in medical sciences. The post was advertised with a rider stating that there could be some research but primarily the successful candidate would head a team of doctors studying the reaction of the human body to galactic space travel.

Note from Catherine Whistler. After barely more than two hours I had a disc handed to me by a smiling Mary Mustow and I slipped it into my handbag. When I got it home and saw the number of pages in the document I wondered just how she had managed to reproduce the work so concisely and quickly. That lady has a very fast mind and puts me to shame I don't mind admitting!

Within two days of that meeting a rather worried looking Don Ford requested a meeting with the Whistler.

"I would like to volunteer if it is permitted for the next jump into the other!" he began. "The Prof suggested that to me when I told him that my irritating cough had returned." He grimaced "I think this time it is more serious than last time!"

"Ok Fordy, get yourself to an offsite doctor say somewhere a good way from here. Ask the Prof if you could go to his doctor in England. That should be fairly secure. And we will do our best to replicate the journey that Heinrich went on. As an afterthought ask Peter if he would be good enough to get himself examined on site here at the same time.

That should make good use of your twin identities, and throw some confusion at the ever present spies. Arrange to come to work for a few days dressed identically, and that should throw a few more hounds off the track!"

"James you are learning; I couldn't have created a better smokescreen myself!" Fordy left looking slightly less worried, as he permitted himself a little smile.

The moment he was out of the door the Whistler clicked his file on Heinrich open, and in addition he looked at all of the pre-flight data for Heinrich's mission to the other. This was still the only manned flight undertaken. He found himself into his robot stance as he tried to get a handle on the shriek that was so clearly recorded on the data and wondered whether he should try to avoid this or recreate it.

For a reason with only the thinnest logical root he decided he should recreate it. He fervently hoped that the issue was rooted in the mass of Heinrich's body which had not been factored in correctly. He studied the maths of the equations and suddenly started as a thought crossed his mind, and spent the next ten minutes scribbling and crossing out. He called Helen in on the internal phone, and twenty seconds later she arrived with her eyebrows raised.

"Just tell me what you think of this" he ordered.

She looked at his hand jottings and said, "Ah, I think that is a better expression for factoring in the human mass!" she paused "just a minute, surely that implies an error in our original equations?"

The Whistler beamed then acquainted her with Fordy's problem. Her mind raced on "Ah, I can see that you want to factor him in correctly and then add a function to account for the mismatch in Heinrich's mission!"

"Indeed I do as that should at least give us some control but I want to force that shriek to happen as I feel sure that somehow it was the conditions that provoked it that set the seal on Heinrich's cure. Insofar as I can ascertain Heinrich felt the pain as the cancer he had was being straightened as he left the rethe and went into the other but there was a shriek as he exited the other. It may not be significant but if it was then we had beginners luck and no mistake! Some of our more recent experiments have shown partial cures for tumours in mice but none are quite as good as the original mouse and Heinrich's"

The Whistler realised that he could emulate a person with a dummy and could now factor a deliberate mass mismatch in an effort to recreate the shriek.

An experiment was done exactly as he decided though several other tasks were made operational whilst in the other just to use the function up and get some data, it took three blasts on the rockets and the shriek was almost exactly recreated as the rethe buster returned to the ether.

Now he had got a handle on it he knew it was possible to avoid the shriek but all of his gut instinct told him to recreate it. Either way a step forward had been made.

Shortly after that a mission was set where the Ford brothers were due to jump to Titan for their games, but the mission commander, none or than doctor Barry was instructed to wait in space whilst Fordy was sent alone into the other. Fordy's mission was to take him directly to the other as it was reasoned that only this would negate his cancer. Other missions with rodents going to different space time continua showed exacerbation or at best partial cure rather than elimination in the undesired condition. He then made his return exactly as planned. Fordy did not find himself feeling mentally better ordered but the cough had subsided, and he complained of a dreadful feeling of needling pain in one of his lungs for a few minutes after the jump to the other had been made.

The Ford brothers and a number of ships crew attended the games on Titan and the flying contest was the highlight.

The winner wore a mask and when this was removed turned out to be a grinning Eric Whistler.

"Privilege of rank!" he smiled at the Fords unspoken question. Eleven shuttles were used to take the visitors down to Titan and three of them were overweight at the start of the return journey. The team's leader radioed back to the mother ship and Doctor Barry sighed as he heard and realised instantly what was going on.

"Ok fasten helmets and exhaust the shuttles air supplies!" he ordered. Before the order was carried out side panelling suddenly detached itself from the walls revealing two old politician prisoners and a woman prisoner. Each in a different ship. The woman prisoner begged the teams to remove the internal panelling in a fourth ship where her baby daughter was discovered.

On hearing this doctor Barry asked the prison authorities for a full manifest of the inmates saying he was in the midst of foiling an attempted breakout. The woman wept openly as the authorities revealed that they had no record of any births there at all.

Back on the mother ship doctor Barry made a mission commander's decision. He decided to repatriate the woman and her daughter but only after a proper investigation. All four stowaways were taken to the bridge where he interviewed the adults both singly and together in his scholarly but quietly determined way.

The woman spat her scorn for the two male prisoners and quite forcefully made allegations of serious misconduct against them saying how both men had been complicit in crimes committed against her and how she would rather be ejected into space with no suit on than spend any time with either of the men. The two ex politicians both became aware that lying was futile and grudgingly admitted what they had done, rather than face ejection into space.

That punishment had been excluded from the general space code but its reputation still hung in the air and struck fear into those who thought they might suffer it.

Doctor Barry radioed that he would send a shuttle containing two shackled men back onto the complex on Titan. "This is an issue solely for you folk down there as this crime has been conceived and committed wholly on Titan, but as we have a baby citizen and her affronted mother in the equation, I have decided to repatriate them and allow the earth authorities to decide their fate." He heard the voices on the other end of the radio mumbling about a year of solitary confinement to be imposed while they made up their minds as what other punishment may be applied. Two dejected men were dropped off on Titan. The mission began its return to earth.

"What will happen to us now?" asked the woman.

"Well firstly I recommend that you spend three days in the giddy room to re-establish your strength against full earth weight then ultimately that will depend on the authorities" smiled Doctor Barry "but you will be treated fairly!"

The woman, whose name was Sara Griffiths, had only been a borderline case for transporting to Titan and anyway had almost served her sentence there.

The two men had been high ranking politicians in the past and had never accepted their fall from grace. They would have no alternative now, after all their most recent behaviour confirmed the justness of their original sentences.

The Ford brothers had thoroughly enjoyed their short stay particularly Peter who was pleased to note that his successor was doing "A good job" as he put it.

Peter Ford was interviewed for his comments on the Titanese set up and had only good things to report.

Back in the space centre, Don Ford was given a savagely detailed medical and no longer had his cough but he did have a strange fresh looking patch on one lung that was nothing like anything else seen before.

So there was still much to learn.

The young baby girl, whose existence had been carefully hidden up to the time of the attempted escape became quite a celebrity and found herself in demand by newshounds as the first Titanese born. Her mother was granted freedom on the basis that the remainder of her sentence was suspended, and she quickly settled in to a near normal life on earth. It couldn't be quite normal with the incessant demands from the media for hers and her daughter's story. Sara had chosen the apt name of Titania for her little girl and this more than anything added to their instant fame. Titania had not yet learnt to speak, but that did not deter the public from wishing to know about her. Sara Griffiths handled the financial aspects of their notoriety with some aplomb as she knew that the media was fickle and would soon cease their interest, but for the moment she knew their immediate future was secure.

Sara made a full and frank statement as to how and when Titania had been conceived and born, and how the little girl's existence had been carefully shrouded from the authorities

She complained bitterly as to how the politicians had used her criminal record plus knowledge of some additional misdemeanours to blackmail her into submitting to their vices. The statement was duly despatched back to Titan along with a few acid comments from Peter Ford. The last I read of the two fallen politicians was that there stay on Titan had been increased indefinitely. Venus was deeply concerned and wrote to Sara Griffiths asking if she could come and see Titania when she was a little older on the grounds that they had their births linked by a common factor, both being done entirely away from earth.

Note from Catherine Whistler: with all of the effort that has gone into time travel research, I am surprised that the Whistler has given it up, though I must say that quite a number of the top wallahs seem to be relieved. Whether he has really given it up or not remains to be seen. Perhaps it is time now to end this book. I don't like ending on an anti climax but really I can't see what else I can do. As we read and file the space reports, if there is anything at all that I find will hang together as a part of this story then I will write about it. There are a number of unfinished love stories unfolding and though I would really like to write about them, they would be a departure from Grandad's original notion. Doctor Barry has a small boy impishness to his character these days. I wonder why?! Until I write something else, good reading and good bye!

Has James Whistler really given time travel up or has he got another idea? He did say privately to me that though there was no longer an official project for time travel he had no objection to any of his team, or anyone else for that matter pursuing time travel ideas, and he would even allot a small budget to any likely ideas that came up.

<u>Addendum by Catherine Whistler</u>:

About five years later I unearthed a report that showed that a completely clandestine operation had been carried out. This was done openly and yet cleverly hidden in the midst of techno jargon, so well that even I had not realised what the significance of the reports were when they arrived. Just for once I was ahead of Jane Johnson when I tumbled to just what had been done.

In essence once the existence of multiple spatial continua had been discovered, the Whistler and Smed had constructed a triangular barbell rethe buster ship very similar to the one used to establish the fact of multiple existences. The only difference was that the new ship was given the ability to spin in any plane whilst it was in the rethe and could thus exit at any desired continuum. Doing a double jump enabled the time shift to be programmed into the first jump and then the earth time zone to be re-entered with the second jump. When this was executed in this manner a time shift of any amount could be programmed in and the spinning ship could be arranged to go to any time zone, in earth's existence. The view as seen from the ship and recorded was ghostly and unclear as the ship was present but not linked exactly to the chosen time zone. At a stroke the Whistler knew that he had found an explanation for the appearance of flying saucers. The ship had done predetermined journeys to leave a camera running to give an earth's eye view of itself as it was operating say a week later. It was evident that the spinning spaceship was translucent but was still visible and as such looked like a flying saucer. Unfortunately all of the data garnered by the ship itself was self deleting as the ship re-entered its own time zone and thus no useful data could be retrieved. The only thing that was not lost was the flying saucer imagery that was produced and the Whistler had sent a mission far into the future and could conclude that there still really was a future and that earth did not destroy itself. Once he knew this he realised that it was unlikely to produce any usable data and decided to close that branch of research but only after several failed attempts to garner data with different types of computor memory. He also confirmed his idea that the random linkages through the rethe could produce odd views of the past such as when folk would swear that they had seen a ghostly roman legion at the bottom of their garden. These folk were not mad or even over imaginative; they did see what they saw but at last an explanation had been found, just as in Newton's time an explanation for rainbows had been discovered with experiments carried out on a prism.

The one good thing that came about as a result of this was the ability to send radio communications to stellar 2 and to any ship away on the other end of a jump. The spinning spaceship had a brief but tenuous link into all other time zones in its spin axis and while the link was there just for a brief instant signals could be transmitted and received. In effect the spin re-introduced time into the rethe, and neatly side stepped Judder's early day's prediction about the incompatibility of frequencies requiring cycles per second into a region where time had no domain. The amount of data at first seemed hopelessly scrambled but using a background pilot signal with a marker pulse permitted synchronising of the spin ships sent into the rethe. It was arranged that two ships would be in the rethe, one at a black portal and one at a blue portal, then signals could be transmitted almost as it could through the ether, but without the signal degradation or time delay caused by long distances. It had been discovered by the triple mission when all three ships had been in the ether simultaneously as they tried to avoid a collision with FB1 that radio transmissions were possible. However later experiments had been singularly unsuccessful in this regard until the advent of the synchronised spinning.

It had taken some time but radio transmission had caught up! When I say spinning ships, these were only small in size and did not cost the unimaginable sums of money required in the production of the Space Adventurer and her sister ships. Earth was very pleased with this development.

Relatively easy communications were established with Stellar 2 and Earth watched fascinated as the pioneers began the long task of opening their world up. The premature ageing did not in the final analysis appear to be true. It was an illusion created by time compression and extension in the early days of rethe travel.

It turned out that the mouse, Fordy and Heinrich had been fortunate. Of all the possibilities that existed regarding transitioning the rethe, only one would give a good result, and that was ether to other and back. One never to be repeated experiment using two mice showed that their DNA's did indeed suffer entanglement so much so that upon return to earth we had two piebald mice instead of a black one and a white one. Neither mouse seemed in any way distressed but neither lived very long after wards. So a universal cure-all was not on.

The time tearing shriek did not in fact seem to enter into the equation for a cancer cure. After all there was no shriek when the mouse went on its unscheduled trip. It took a while but small rodents were sent through to the other and without a shriek they did well after their return. Fame came unexpectedly to one man as the shriek became known as the 'juddering time rip.'

Adam Round presented these findings to the world and due largely to his style of presentation the space centre was not swamped with people clamouring for a cure for cancer. Very few folk were strong enough minded to allow a machine to govern what little future they had left. No-one liked the idea of going into the rethe and through into the other completely unaccompanied as there really was a serious risk of oblivion. Desperation in the later stages of the unfortunates afflicted did result in a number of volunteers but by that stage they were so ill that the journey into normal space would certainly have killed them, and so the numbers of people attempting the cure were miniscule, and the success rate was only moderate. The mouse, Heinrich and Fordy had entered the other whilst they were still in the early stages of a disease and thus the repair work required was relatively small. In Heinrich's case it has since been surmised that he may have also had an undetected form of brain tumour in its very early stages. When this was cured a side effect was that his mind seemed and is still better ordered than before.

Both Fordy and Heinrich have remained in good health so there must be room for expansion in this field sooner or later.

One other strange and not tightly connected piece of data was that though nearly all data was lost when transferring between time zones, the image of a moustachioed man some times appeared. I had no idea who it was but the Prof gasped saying "I remember my dad going on about him, it looks like Lord Lucan to me! He disappeared after getting into a spot of financial pickle and other alleged crimes, so perhaps he and others had slipped through a time gate of some sort, no wonder the authorities couldn't find him when they wanted to!"

Research along medical lines is quietly continuing but really the main thrust is now the production of robots for use on inhospitable stellar bodies.

Heinrich's remark about the Prof and captain Johnson being the first to get through the rethe turned out to be accurate after a further more informed examination of the flight data, but neither man has wished to lay claim to the fact. That whole episode was riddled with chance and as an experiment could not be repeated due to the uncontrolled approach unknowingly adopted at the time. The Prof was quite content to bask in the knowledge that he got into the rethe and safely back out. He says his blood runs cold when he considers that his suggestion might have caused and reversed a double jump. In his wisdom he knows that he is lucky to be around to talk about it, and he is still uncomfortable when he considers that his suggestion might have caused 18000 crew deaths including his own. One conclusion drawn by the Prof was that Captain Johnson had kept his rocket motors at full thrust as they went into the rethe and left them going for a while before shutting them down. Helens theory of inverse time function should have meant that their rocket stayed in the rethe for an infinite amount of time, because the rocket motors would have been trying to escape back to the ether. It escaped the rethe but got into the other, then somehow got back again. It will take a very brave man to attempt to recreate this action, and the Whistler has no intention of asking for volunteers. Helen's inverse time function was still explained as if one considers going into the other, in effect you would be lost in the other and thus never again expected in the rethe and thence into the ether. Research in the form of theorising is continuing along this route because it does mean that a trip into the other can be done by any ship capable of reaching close to warp factor one. The Whistler however likes to have a handle on control and the multi existence traversing ships give him that. Somebody will present a reason for using this simple approach without doubt but it isn't likely to be yet awhile.

The space exploration now has an excellent chance of continuing at a rapid pace but I think that this story of the early pioneering efforts is just about done.

Right now I'm off to doctor Barry's marriage to Mary Mustow so I think the time has come to draw a final line under the story begun by my grandfather, and thus I am signing off permanently,– I think! Best regards Catherine Whistler.

An original story; by DAVID DONALD KEIRLE, July 2011. The author acknowledges that his ideas have been influenced by what he has read over the years and thanks all those who have gone before.

ABOUT THE AUTHOR

The author was born in 1940, during the dark days of the war. Nevertheless, he enjoyed a good childhood and a reasonable education, culminating in grammar school and, finally, technical college, where he studied as an electrical engineer, travelling the world as part of his duties.

Retiring in 2005, he decided to see if he had a book in him, the results of which are now laid before you in the form of a trilogy.

CPSIA information can be obtained
at www.ICGtesting.com
Printed in the USA
FFOW04n1439100217
32257FF